Neysa —

One could not wish for
a better friend. You a
treasure. Love, Sydney

TONE DEAD

ALSO BY SYDNEY PRESTON

Too Late for Redemption

TONE DEAD

A Britannia Bay Mystery

SYDNEY PRESTON

RYE PUBLICATIONS

This is a work of fiction. Names, places, characters and incidents either are the product of the author's imagination or are used fictitiously, and any resemblance to actual persons, living or dead, business establishments, events, or locales is entirely coincidental.

Rye Publications
212 Fourth Avenue West
Qualicum Beach, BC
V9K 1S3

Printed and Bound in Canada by Printorium Bookworks

ISBN: 978-1-7753157-2-8 (trade paperback)
ISBN: 978-1-7753157-3-5 (e-book)

Cast of Permanent Characters in the Series

Detective Sergeant Jimmy Tan

Wife, Ariel

Rossini Family

Detective Sergeant Ray Rossini
Wife, Georgina
Children, Marcus and Gabriella
Umberto and Silvana Rossini, Ray's parents and owners of Catalani Italian Ristorante

Britannia Bay Police Department – Day Shift Personnel

Chief William Wyatt. Wife, Sherilee
Detective Sergeant and SOCO, Josh Atkins
Constables: Adam Berry, Craig Carpenter, Dalbir Dhillon, Tamsyn Foxcroft, Mike Heppner, Gene McDaniel, Tim Novak, Simon Rhys-Jones
Special Municipal Constable and Media Liaison, Marina Davidova
Dispatchers, Mary-Beth McKay, Robyn Lewitski

R.C.M.P.

Corporal Ike Griffin

Coroner/Medical Officer

Dr. Dayani Nayagam

Britannia Bay Residents

Clive Abernathy, President of Heritage Gardens Society. He and his wife Daphne, own Charterhouse B&B
Justine Hughes, owner of Justine's Joint café
Keith Kittridge, editor of *The Britannia Bay Bugle*. Wife, Edith
Delilah Moore, neighbour of the Tans
Pieter Verhagen, Mayor
Lana Westbrook, neighbour of the Tans and Pastry Chef for Catalani's

- - -

A note to readers: For "Tone Dead" only, Russian last names have male and female forms. An "a" is generally added to female names. So it is not an error when you see Stepanov and Stepanova. When referring to the family, the male form takes precedence. That is why you will read, "the Stepanovs."

Denn alles Fleisch es ist wie Gras und alle Herrlichkeit des Menschen wie des Grases Blumen. Das Gras ist verdorret und die Blume abgefallen

- Ein Deutches Requiem
Johannes Brahms

For all flesh is as grass, and all the glory of man as the flower of grass. The grass withereth, and the flower thereof falleth away.

- 1st Peter 1:24
Holy Bible, King James Version

Prologue

She lay still, connected to a drip and heart monitor. The doctor and her children thought she couldn't hear them and understand what they were saying. But she could. Some part of her understood. She had always had a good brain. But was it her brain comprehending their words? Or was it Mikhail interpreting them and conveying their underlying message? He was there with her. She could sense his presence.

They said her cognitive function had been compromised by the massive blood clot. And her heart, already weak, had suffered a mild coronary. She would most likely remain in a coma for some time. And when she recovered, she might be paralyzed or unable to speak. And—in hushed tones—there was the possibility of dementia.

Did she even want to recover with what was awaiting her? Being unable to walk or to speak? Unable to recognize her children or grandchildren? Never able to sing a note again? No. A life like that held no charm for her. What enjoyment could she wring out of a few moments of lucidity? Why stay when Mikhail was waiting for her?

One

March 1st

The March lion arrived, unleashing its rage, howling through the night and dashing down icy sheets of sleet this way and that. Barometers and temperatures dove in tandem. February's final balmy days of a promised early spring had been a deceit, a cruel mirage. The barking of sea lions in the bay was the only sound that could be heard above the tumult.

Buffeted by gusts as he walked to work, Detective Sergeant Jimmy Tan dodged fronds of cedar and fir sent flying by the capricious wind. The air bit his nose. His peaked cap kept his face somewhat shielded, but needles of ice pricked the nape of his neck, convincing him to pull up the collar of the thick duty jacket. Despite the foul weather, he felt content, perhaps due to the general peace that had settled on the town after the first and only homicide two years before. The murder had shaken the small community primarily because the person slain had been a well-known land developer from a prominent family. It struck even closer to home for Jimmy, as the victim had been his and Ariel's neighbour.

There was a newer concern for the townsfolk, however. Low-level crime was on the rise, credited to a homeless shelter and halfway house that had taken over a vacated elementary school. For the first time anyone could remember, people were locking their cars and homes and installing alarm systems. But this was not something that kept Jimmy awake at nights. He knew that, overall, it was a safe village.

The residents liked to call it a village, which caused Mayor Pieter Verhagen to blanch whenever he heard the word. It was a town, and to him, any diminution of the designation was an affront to his position. As it was, it had been a major victory convincing Council to change Reeve to Mayor. In his mind, "Reeve" sounded country-bumpkinish. While managing to prevail in this battle, there was nothing he could do about the street names, which he thought would be more at home amongst the pages of children's story books.

In the 1940s, when it became customary to alphabetize street names after trees and flowers, some of the decisions led to fisticuffs in the old community hall. Each time a new street was carved out of the district, people prepared for repercussions. In 2000, a collective sigh could be heard when the district manager announced that no more streets could be fit within the town's boundaries.

The only alteration took place in 1984, the year *Nightmare on Elm Street* appeared on the screen. A new name had to be chosen to replace *their* Elm Street, inevitably leading to more arguments. It was finally decided that Evergreen would be more appropriate as there were no elm trees in the region, while evergreens were everywhere.

As Jimmy approached the police station, he watched intrepid seniors rushing out of the rain and into Bayside Foods for the early bird breakfast special. The cheap price was a lost leader—an enticement for people to spend more time inside to buy groceries.

When he stepped through the station entrance, Mary Beth McKay, one of the front desk personnel, looked up. "My gosh, Jimmy! Did you walk?"

"It's only a couple of blocks."

"But you're drenched." She buzzed him into the squad room.

"It's some storm, all right. Any trees down in your area?"

"Nothing major. Just a few branches here and there. What about your place?"

"So far, so good." He looked around. Constables Tamsyn Foxcroft and Simon Rhys-Jones were at their work stations and gave him a wave. He saw no sign of his partner. "Ray not in yet?" he asked Mary Beth.

"He's down in the parking garage with his new toy," she giggled. "He's like a kid in a candy store."

"Guess I'll go see what mischief he's up to." Hanging up his wet jacket in the locker room, he bounded down the steps to the garage, where he found Ray Rossini in the driver's seat of a sixteen-foot Mobile Crime Vehicle, fiddling with the retractable phone cradle.

"Look what the cat dragged in."

"I think all the weather experts are correct," he teased. "It's climate change."

Ray bit, throwing him a look of disgust. "Yeah. Right. And Santa Claus is a Communist."

Jimmy laughed. They had been down this road before.

Ray returned to his current interest. "We're gonna have to take a course in how to use this baby," he griped, pointing to the high-tech dashboard.

The arrival of the vehicle came as a result of the mayor finally admitting to how poorly equipped the station had been during the murder investigation. Chagrined and nudged by town pride, the mayor had let out the ties of his tightly bound purse and agreed to bring the department into the 21st century, but reeled when he saw the price. For many weeks, he and his Chief Financial Officer struggled to find cuts in order to accommodate the purchase.

5

"It's so complicated," Ray said. "Look at all these screens, and every one of them is for something different. It's like a bloody cockpit. Who've we got that can figure it out?"

"Dalbir might be able to do it. He has a teenager who could probably hack into the federal government."

Ray grunted. "Some four-year-olds are way ahead of me. They're talking rockets when I'm just figuring out the wheel." He heaved his bulk out of the seat. "Check this out," he said, taking a few steps and opening a door. "Our own john."

"That'll be a welcome change."

"Yeah. No more pissing behind a bush. And look at this fridge. Big enough for sandwiches and stuff."

"Don't forget evidence bags."

"There's plenty of space for them."

"Where's the forensic gear?"

Ray opened a cupboard where shelves were crammed with individual packets containing white suits, shoe covers, masks, and latex gloves. "The SOCOs are gonna be over the moon." He closed the door and pointed to another section. "And how about this? A place for Gene's photography. Just think. Processing evidence right at the scene." He sighed. "We'll probably never have another homicide to see what it can really do."

Jimmy shook his head. "Don't tempt Fate."

Two

Irina Stepanova felt the stiffness in her early morning bones as she made her way out of her grandmother suite and into the kitchen of the spacious house, her watchful caregiver, Lyudmila, as always by her side. Her son, Grigory, and daughter-in-law, Monique, were seated side-by-side at the booth eating breakfast and whispering in animated conversation. Seeing Irina, they hushed up, and Grigory quickly thrust something behind him.

"Good morning, Mama," they chimed.

"Good morning, darlings." Preoccupied with her own bodily concerns, she did not notice her son's furtive movement.

Lyudmila slid a chair out from under a small table and waited while the elderly woman settled herself, then pushed it in. Irina preferred to eat at the table rather than the breakfast nook, which she found too difficult to shift around. Moreover, the table top was too high for her tiny frame. She shook a napkin onto her lap.

"Did you sleep well?" Monique asked.

"As well as could be expected, with all these kinks and knots," she said, more bitterly than intended. Hearing her tone, she sweetened it with a smile. Lyudmila brought over her normal breakfast—a pot of strong tea, honey, and two *botterbrots*.

Irina inspected the open-faced sandwiches, pleased at the toppings of ham with thinly sliced cucumber on one and sliced hard-boiled eggs and fish roe on the other. She glanced up at her children, for indeed she thought of Monique as her own flesh and blood after thirty years of marriage to her son. "You're late leaving this morning," she noted.

They began to ease their way out of the nook. "We were waiting for the storm to die down," Monique told her. "We're going now." When they came over to her, Irina lifted her cheek for the customary kiss.

"What are you working on today?"

"The first movement of the Schubert 13," Grigory replied.

"Ah, the *Rosamunde*. So heartbreaking."

"And I have a student at six o'clock," Monique said. "We may or may not be home before you leave for choir practice."

Irina flipped a hand. "It doesn't matter, dear. No doubt we'll meet as ships do."

Monique kissed her cheek. "Love you, Mama."

"I know you do, *lapochka*." She felt her eyes begin to smart. "Now, off you go."

Lyudmila removed their dishes and tidied the area. Finding *The Bayside Bugle* tucked behind one of the cushions, she brought it over and laid it on Irina's table. After pouring the tea, she returned to her chores.

Irina added two teaspoons of honey to her tea and prepared to enjoy her meal while reading the paper. A few minutes passed. She took another bite of the bread and chewed slowly while reading. As she sipped her strong, sweet tea, her eyes flew open. A sudden intake of breath caused drops of hot liquid to enter her lungs sending her into fits of coughing.

"Madam!" Lyudmila rushed over. She quickly hoisted Irina, bent her over the chair back and thumped her as hard as advisable fearing for her frail bones. The woman was big and strong, and aware of her strength.

"Enough," Irina squeaked, righting herself. Lyudmila held out a clean tissue. Irina wiped her eyes then blew her nose. "Thank you," she said, regaining what dignity she could. She held out the newspaper, rustling the pages toward her housekeeper. "No wonder I choked. Look at this."

With trepidation, Lyudmila took the paper from Irina's shaking hand, removed her reading glasses from her apron pocket and read the article. It was a review of a chamber music performance given by Beyond Baroque, the string quartet Monique had founded and in which Grigory played second violin. The writer could barely contain her contempt for classical music.

As she read, Lyudmila realized that the odd location of the paper hadn't been a mistake. Grigory and Monique hadn't wanted Irina to see it. The mistake had been Lyudmila's for placing it in front of Irina.

"That Diane Drake is a cretin," Irina spat out, tapping the offending article. "She is tone deaf."

Lyudmila handed the paper back. "I'm sorry, Madam. I think you were not meant to see it. I found it behind a cushion."

Irina patted her hand. "Never mind, dear. I would have seen it eventually. Perhaps they wanted to break it to me more gently." She took another sip of tea. "Will you please make me another pot? This has gone cold." Returning to the paper, she read a long, glowing review of a blue grass band accompanied by pictures of dancing audience members. She felt a stab of pain in her chest. Her breathing quickened. Blood began pounding in her ears. "Lyudmila . . ." she croaked.

Lyudmila, recognizing the symptoms, picked up Irina as though she were one of her cleaning cloths, and carried her into the living room where she placed her on the sofa. After filling a glass of water, she held Irina's head and made her take small sips. "Did you take your beta blocker this morning?"

"No," she replied weakly.

"Hold this." She handed the water to Irina, ran to the en suite, and grabbed the prescription. Shaking out one of the capsules, she returned and watched while Irina swallowed it down. "Breathe slowly," she ordered. Taking a lemon from the fridge, she cut it into quarters. Irina saw the small bowl in Lyudmila's hand and knew the drill. She began sucking on the pieces, alternating with small sips of water until all that remained was pulp.

Within an hour Irina felt fine. The remedies had done what they were supposed to do, and Lyudmila had done what she was hired to do—look after her charge.

Irina couldn't afford to be incapacitated. Too many people were depending on her. Thank God she had Lyudmila to rely on. Now who could she depend on for a fair preview of their upcoming concert? She didn't want that Drake woman coming anywhere near her choir. Perhaps it was time to call the editor.

Three

Diane Drake dragged herself out of bed, head heavy, eyes puffed. Six hours of sleep after three small glasses of wine didn't cut it anymore. She needed more of one and less of the other. She was afraid alcohol would tear down her protective wall, have her saying things that had to remain unsaid. At least she hadn't slept through her alarm. Missing her daily seven o'clock check-in would have set God knows what in motion. She picked up her encrypted cellphone, spoke the brief words, then stumbled to the bathroom.

Feeling close to normal after a shower and shampoo, she dressed, then placed bread in the toaster oven and dropped a pod in her coffee machine. While waiting for them to respectively brown and brew, she turned on her laptop. Scrolling through her e-mail, she spotted a message notifying her of the monthly bank transfer from her rented condo in Edmonton. Picking up the same cellphone, she texted a message and received a reply an instant later. Her heart sank. It meant more time stuck in this backwater. Damn! Why hadn't she just walked away and left the body lying there?

Four

Keith Kittridge hung up the phone and sighed. Irina Stepanova's words might have been spoken softly, but they were edged in steel. Hearing that Diane Drake was doing a disservice to the community with her negative articles, Keith's ears pricked up.

When the offer of a replacement for former reporter Malcolm MacDonald had been dropped in his lap two years before, he thought his problem was solved. The paper was being threatened with a lawsuit for another of MacDonald's flights of fancy, and Keith's only recourse was to fire him. Wondering where on earth he was going to find another reporter willing to move to a small town and work on a tri-weekly paper for peanuts had led to many sleepless nights.

Then came the call that was his saving grace, or so it seemed. Now, though, Diane was becoming trouble as well. Reading the several reviews Irina had been mentioning, he grimaced. They bordered on being nasty. He picked up the latest issue and strode into the production room.

Diane's head was down, composing another review or preview of yet another concert. He knew there was a lot on offer in the area. His wife, Edith, was always traipsing off to at least one a week with her friends.

"Diane!" he bellowed in his gravelly voice.

Flinching, she looked up, a question on her face. It was a pretty face with "good bones"—features that would last into old age. The only down side was the wariness in her grey-green eyes. Keith wondered if they had always been so watchful or was it simply a manifestation of her present situation.

"What?"

"I've just had a call from Irina Stepanova. She gave me an earful about how you're covering the classical music scene. Accused you of being biased against good music."

"Yeah. What *she* calls good music. I *do* have an appreciation for good music. Just not classical music. Most of it leaves me cross-eyed."

He secretly agreed with her, but couldn't be on her side in this skirmish. "Your reviews are cleverly written, but sometimes they aren't very kind. You have to think about how hard it is for musical groups in a small community. There are only so many people they can lure in. It's different if you're running a pub and have live bands—like this other review you did." He held open the paper to the appropriate page. "And when it's on the page before the sour one about a chamber music performance—given by Irina's children, I might add—it stands out. You have to be more even handed."

Diane shrugged "Okay. I'll grit my teeth and do it."

"Good, because you still have to do a preview of their concert next month." One problem sorted, he thought. Now all he had to do was find another dozen advertisers so that he could pay the bills. Something else that kept him awake.

Five

Lana Westbrook watched as Gabriella Rossini carefully packed up the cannoli in a white pastry box and tied it with string. It was now time for Lana to untie strings of her own. "Gabby, I've been thinking about something for a while."

"That sounds serious," the teenager said as she removed her hair net.

"Well, it is, in a way. I've taught you almost everything I know. So, you really don't need to come for lessons anymore."

Gabby's face fell. "Oh ..."

It wasn't the reaction Lana was expecting. She thought the teenager would be thrilled. "To tell you the truth, I've just embellished the last few things we've done because I enjoy having you here."

"I enjoy it, too," Gabby said. She liked the tall, sophisticated woman with her angled cap of chestnut hair and huge brown eyes. She had learned much more than baking from her. What the world was like outside of Britannia Bay, for one thing. "So, what do I do now?"

"Well, for one thing, you're ready to bake the Italian pastries for Catalani's."

Her jaw dropped. "You mean, like, take your job?"

Lana laughed. "Not my whole job, but part of it. If your mother agrees, that is. You could handle that from their kitchen, and I would continue baking the lemon pies and chocolate cakes here. They keep me busy enough." Truth be told, she needed some time off. She had been working almost non-stop since arriving in Britannia Bay six years ago. It was time for a break. Time to visit her parents in San Francisco. Maybe go back to Paris for a few weeks and see old friends.

"How do you feel about that?"

"Um. Okay I guess."

"Then I'll talk to your mother about it." Lana looked out the front window, her brow furrowing as Gabriella put on her coat. "It's awful out there, Gabby. I'll drive you to the restaurant."

A dash of consternation flew across the girl's face. "Oh, no. That's okay. I'll walk. I don't mind," she replied hastily, shaking her head. "I have an umbrella."

After a quick hug, Lana watched through the window as Gabriella and her umbrella bent into the wind and pushed down the street. As Lana was about to turn back to the kitchen, the sound of loud mufflers caught her ear. Looking out, she saw a shiny black vintage two-door car with garish orange and red flames painted along the side pull up beside Gabriella. The girl opened the passenger door and got in. Lana wondered who he was and why Gabriella hadn't told her she was being picked up. *Should I tell Georgina? If I were a mother, I would want to be aware of this.*

Although it was bitterly cold, the promised snow had still failed to show, much to the delight of Mayor Verhagen, whose snow-removal budget was already in the red from last season's record-setting accumulation. In fact, the entire budget was on life support with only a few weeks until the end of the fiscal year. He blamed that on the excessive cost of the police department's latest purchase.

Escaping his chambers, he ran across the square to Justine's Joint for a cup of herbal tea and a Danish. The place was nearly empty. Only a few brave souls were out and about. He sat quietly, thinking about ways to cut costs and worrying his little change purse with his fingers.

It must be serious, Justine thought. *It looks like he's planning to pay me.* Verhagen's stinginess was legendary, and on more than one occasion he had to be chastised to pony up when it came to paying for his personal expenditures at pubic venues.

As she watched him, the door to the café flew open and banged the wall. Startled, everyone looked up to see an old woman struggling to enter with her grocery-laden walker. Verhagen, recognizing a P.R. moment, jumped up, helped her inside then wrestled the door back into position. "Are you all right, Mrs. Moore?"

"No worse for the wear, Mr. Mayor," the woman sing-songed. "And thank you."

"You're entirely welcome," he said in his politician's voice. "It's my pleasure to help one of our favourite sen . . . ah . . . citizens." He knew her opinion on references to age. "Old is a dirty three-letter word," he had heard her say more than once.

Delilah Moore choked off a caustic reply, choosing to ignore his sugary words. He, after all, had offered her a non-paying position on the Town Enhancement Committee. It allowed her to go wherever she wished to root out problems she thought needed attention. She relished the job, especially as it gave her an opportunity to squelch too much jibber-jabber at Council meetings and to lock horns with Vivian Hoffmeyer. Nothing pleased her more than throwing cold water on the so-called President of the Britannia Bay Horticultural Society. Whenever Delilah heard that name, she wanted to snort. And often did. She had no time for hoity-toity self-promoters.

Today, however, her mind was on another problem that needed

fixing—fast. She had seen something that upset her, and as soon as she had warmed up, she was going to hightail it home and get to it.

Verhagen wondered about inviting her to sit with him. If he offered her a place at his table, would she expect him to foot the bill for whatever she ordered? Before he could decide, she sank into a chair across from him.

"It's so cold out there. My feet are like ice. I don't think I could make it home without a cup of hot chocolate." She raised her eyebrows and gave the mayor a mischievous smile.

That's not too bad, he thought. "Why don't I get that for you?"

"And ask Justine to put extra whipping cream in it. I don't want those little marshmallows. They take too long to melt."

When the mayor returned with Delilah's hot chocolate, she thanked him, then blew on it, inadvertently flicking little fluffs of whipped cream onto the table. "Oh, shoot!" She grabbed a napkin and wiped them off. The mayor, who was also noted for his fastidiousness, had instinctively shot back in his chair and checked for any spots on his coat. Being none, he relaxed.

Delilah laughed. "A little bit of whipped cream won't kill you, Pieter. It might make you sweet . . . er." She took a sip. "Mmm. Anyway, I'm glad I ran into you. I've got an idea on how to bring some cash to the town's coffers."

With the mention of money, he was all ears. One thing he knew—this woman was sharp and full of good ideas. And as this had now become a business meeting, he could put everything on his expense account.

Georgina Rossini was in a good mood as she checked the reservations for the evening. With the terrible weather, she was expecting few patrons, but the book was almost full. When the phone rang, she thought it might be a cancellation, but seeing Lana's name on the display, she picked up immediately. "Hi Lana, how are you?"

As Lana hesitantly began to relate her concerns about what she had seen, Georgina's mind zeroed in on what she was saying. Her mood darkened. She didn't like what she was hearing. When Lana appeared to be finished, Georgina finally spoke. "No, you did the right thing, Lana. I'm glad you told me. Gabby has never said anything about a boy. And, no, I won't say anything. I don't want to jeopardize your relationship with her."

Given that opening, Lana mentioned her decision to end Gabby's lessons and why. "You're right. She's a born baker," Georgina said. "I'd be happy to have her do our Italian pastries. But you know, we still have the space problem in the restaurant's kitchen. And our kitchen at home wouldn't pass provincial inspection. You may be stuck with her." She laughed. It was not echoed by Lana.

Sensing Lana's reticence, Georgina did a quick turn around. "Of course, that's something the three of us will have to discuss. It will depend on whether she wants to take on that commitment. That's another thing to consider."

The call ended, but that conversation, no doubt, would continue. The crucial discussion, however, would be about the boy. And when to have it. And with whom? Georgina debated whether to tell Ray. *He might go off half-cocked. Ground Gabby. Better wait. Maybe Marcus knows who this guy is. Sounds like he may be more his age than Gabby's.* She checked her watch. Her son would be in class, so she would have to wait until tomorrow to call him. And her daughter should be arriving in a few minutes. Would Gabby allow some guy to make her late? If so, that would set off warning bells.

When Delilah arrived home, Tabitha jumped down from the sofa where she had been watching out the window at the flying debris. She followed her mistress into the kitchen and hopped up on the table.

Delilah absently petted the tortoise-shell cat while looking up the non-emergency number for the police department. Up until the time of her neighbour's murder, she had been suspicious of the Rossini family. For all she knew, they could be involved with the Cosa Nostra and Ray could be a dirty cop. But the investigation convinced her that he was on the up-and-up. She put her suspicions down to her love of TV police dramas. Now she was concerned about one member of that family. Finding the number, she picked up the phone and made the call.

Six

Ariel Tan leaned close to the singer next to her. "Shh," she whispered. Phileda Bagshaw simply did not know when to shut up. Her constant nattering put Ariel on edge. Not only did she never seem to know where they were in the score, but it was just plain rude. There was Irina, trying her best to turn fish chowder into bouillabaisse, with few diners giving the chef the respect she deserved.

Now Ariel had missed what Irina was trying to impart to the singers, most of whom had no musical training. In her opinion, Irina should be given a medal for founding this choir and regularly putting on a decent performance of a major musical composition. The *Deutsches Requiem* by Brahms was a beautiful but demanding score requiring subtle dynamics. Ariel had worried that the members would balk at singing in German, let alone pronouncing it correctly. Many were older Brits who still had vivid memories of the hardships and deprivation during and after the Second World War. Ariel, herself, loved singing in German, but she had had the benefit of performing solo recitals with gorgeous melodies by Schubert, Wolf, Mahler and other lieder composers.

Irina nodded to the rehearsal pianist, and they picked up where they left off. Just as suddenly, she stopped. "No! No! I am still hearing 'why lyblick.' It is 'vee leebleech.' For that *ch* put the edges of the back of your tongue on your top teeth." She demonstrated and had the choir practice. "Now, please mark your score. And remember, the second vowel of the ie and ei combination is the one you pronounce. There are many instances of i before e and e before i. Mark them all." She let out a long sigh. "Now, let's begin again."

At the break, Irina signaled for the choir manager, Graham Palmer, to join her while people drifted off to grab a drink, gossip and stretch. As Ariel passed by the two of them, she caught part of their conversation and saw them reading a page of *The Bayside Bugle*. Hearing a gasp, she turned back to see Irina collapsing.

"Get Perry!" Graham shouted, laying a moaning Irina across an upholstered pew. Seconds later, Perry Allingham, baritone and cardiologist, rushed back into the auditorium. Noting her shortness of breath and perspiration, he called 9-1-1, explaining the emergency and who he was. The answers Irina had given to his questions convinced him that she was experiencing a mild heart attack. He knew she was already on beta blockers.

Ariel pulled Graham aside. "Do you have Grigory's number?"

He looked at her, dazed, then realized what she was saying. "Yes. I do. I'll call him right now." He stepped aside, but kept his eyes on Irina.

Choir members stood in little groups, worry etched on their faces. Irina was old and frail. It was no secret that she had health issues, but she had more endurance than many of the younger people present. Even her voice was youthful. That was chalked up to her years of correct vocal technique.

The ambulance arrived. While Irina was being examined by the paramedics, Ariel was checking out one of them. *Was that Pascal*

Nadeau, Lana's former gardener? She had heard Lana say that he had been a paramedic when the Lac Megantic train disaster happened in his home town. Thoroughly shaken by what he had seen, he left his job *and* Québec and moved across the country, as though space would diminish the memories. But after an incident involving Delilah two years before, he decided to return to his former profession. Ariel would tell Lana that she had seen him carrying out his duties with care and attentiveness. It was the only highlight of the evening.

Graham came up to her. "Grigory and Monique are on their way to the hospital."

"What are we going to do if she can't carry on?"

"Grigory may know someone. He has contacts everywhere. The problem would be raising the money to pay him or her." Then a thought occurred to him. "I'll have to tell the soloists. They were donating their time because of their connections to Irina."

Ariel's face fell. "If they pull out, we'll have to hire new ones and pay them."

"Let's not jump too far ahead, Ariel. We should know more by tomorrow or in a few days."

Ariel nodded. Choir members were already gathering up their belongings and leaving. She soon joined them.

"You're home early," Jimmy said, looking up from a book, Roger purring on his lap, Molly curled on the adjacent chair. He saw something in Ariel's face and rose abruptly, shocking the long-haired black cat out of his transcendental meditation, and dumped him unceremoniously onto the floor. The Siamese leapt down before the same thing happened to her.

"Oh, Jimmy," she cried. "Irina's had a heart attack. She's in the hospital."

"Oh, God. That's awful." As soon as his sympathetic words were out of his mouth, her pent-up tears spilled over. He put his arms around her and she wept into his shirt. He softly kissed her curls and rubbed her back. After a minute, she became quiet but remained there, wrapped in his love. "I'll make you some cocoa," he said. "You go and get into your jammies and if you want to talk about it, we will."

She reluctantly extricated herself from his embrace and looked him full in the face. "Jimmy Tan. You are the most wonderful man in the whole universe."

He smiled. "I know."

She gave him a poke. The moment evaporated

Ray was sawing Douglas firs by the time Georgina finally made it to bed. For once, his sonorous snoring wasn't the reason for her being unable to sleep. It was Gabby, who *had* shown up at Catalani's close to the designated time, but with an unusual flush on her face. And she had been distracted. It took more time than usual for her to set the tables and prepare the pastry cart, adding her day's creations in the process. The most troubling part for Georgina was that Gabby's thanks for her mother's proud approval was more off-hand than gracious.

Boys had never been a major part of her daughter's life. She knew that Gabby and her girlfriends sometimes hung out with a group of boys, but none paired up. It was a small high school, given the fact that most of the residents were middle-aged or seniors. There weren't many couples with teenaged children or youngsters.

Georgina wondered again about the driver of the car. She hoped Marcus, now away at college, would come up with a name. With that worry more or less sorted, she managed to fall asleep.

Several miles away, Irina, seeing her beloved husband beckoning to her, breathed her last breath.

Seven

March 2nd

Shortly before dawn, Roger and Molly woke Jimmy with their nightly meanderings. Usually he was able to sleep through them, but this time the added sounds of things pelting the roof shook him awake. The wind was sending things flying: pine cones and branches and whatever else it could find to fling about. He got up and looked out, but could see nothing in the tar-black night. In the kitchen, he checked the small wi-fi weather station. The temperature had plummeted overnight. He began preparing his breakfast.

The cats padded in. While he waited for his coffee to brew, he spooned food into their bowls. Still in their nighttime hunting phase, they remained silent.

After eating and cleaning his dishes, Jimmy showered and dressed. Ariel hadn't budged. Armed as she was with earplugs and an eye mask, she could sleep through a full-blown thunderstorm.

When light appeared in the leaden sky, he peered out again. A counterpane of frost covered everything. He shrugged into his jacket, turned on the outdoor lights and walked gingerly down the driveway, now sparkling like a diamond-encrusted stream. *The Bayside Bugle* had been delivered, protected by a plastic sleeve. Since it was still too early to go to the station, he chose to read and have another cup of coffee. Besides, he didn't like to leave without spending some time with Ariel.

Roger jumped up on his lap. Molly retreated to the bedroom. Jimmy turned to the paper, looking first at the crime report. It was blessedly benign. The clock ticked. The wind howled. Roger purred. Jimmy's head dropped.

Ariel had risen, and upon seeing no Jimmy, tiptoed down the hall, Molly trailing behind her. She stopped at the serene kitchen scene and smiled. The newspaper chose that moment to slowly slide from Jimmy's hands and plop to the floor. Roger scooted down. Jimmy awoke with a start. Ariel laughed, came over and kissed his cheek. "What are you doing up so early? And dressed already."

"The wind woke me up. You're up early, too." He looked at her tousled hair, the corkscrew curls heading off in different directions.

A sudden gust slammed into the house. She jumped. "This weather is beginning to get on my nerves."

"If we get some moisture, it could bring snow."

"Oh, charming. Well, I have no place to go today, so I'll just hunker down with the cats."

By mid-morning, the unrelenting wind had torn the remaining clouds to shreds leaving behind a bright but brittle day. The snow remained on hold.

Ariel was at the piano going over the Brahms when Graham called. Hearing his quavering voice, she took in a quick breath knowing what was coming. As he struggled to tell her the news, she felt his loss deeply. His friendship with Irina had been deep and enduring. He would be devastated.

"There's something else, Ariel. I've notified the soloists and unfortunately neither one wants to proceed now. They were doing it gratis because of their long connection with Irina."

Ariel slumped. "So does that mean cancelling the concert?"

"Not necessarily." He paused "Actually, I was wondering if you would like to take the soprano solo." His tentativeness made her smile. How could he possibly know that she had dreamed of doing this movement?

"Oh, Graham. I would *love* to do it! Thank you for that vote of confidence."

"Oh, that's a relief, Ariel. You'll be great."

"But what about the baritone?"

"I think Perry might do a good job of it. He's a fine singer."

"But what about you? You could do it ,now that you're a baritone."

He took a few beats before replying gravely. "I wouldn't be able to carry it off, Ariel."

She understood.

"I'll call the choir together for Saturday morning to give them an update. Grigory is going to ask around for a conductor. So, lots to think about and do. It'll keep me busy and maybe take my mind off . . ." his voice faded.

Ariel felt her heart lurch. After he ended the call, she wondered who would comfort him. There was gossip about his wife being jealous of Irina's importance in his life. If it were true, Ariel wasn't certain the comfort would come from her. At one time, Graham had been a strapping and handsome man, and a desired leading tenor on the operatic stage. He still attracted women with his habit of locking his deep-set hazel eyes on them while listening intently to their words, no matter how inane. Because of his height, he did tend to lean over, and when he did, a forelock of his thick, white hair would fall nearly to his eyebrows, whose hairs had conflicted notions about their direction.

Her plans to tell Lana about Pascal had now changed. No doubt the somber news about Irina would dominate the conversation. Living life on an even keel was a constant balancing act.

Jimmy was delighted when Ariel told him about the solo. He knew she missed her singing recitals. Teaching voice and being in a choir was not nearly as satisfying as standing in front of an audience and using the gift that God gave you to bring enjoyment to people's faces.

"I hope nothing interferes with you being at the concert," she said.

"That's the Saturday night before Easter Sunday, right?"

"Right."

"No problem. That's usually a quiet weekend."

Eight

March 3rd

Ray and Jimmy sat at one of the small tables in the station's kitchen, drinking coffee and enjoying some of the pastries Gabriella had baked, but didn't think were perfect enough for the patrons of Catalani's.

"These are really good," Jimmy said.

"Yeah, she's a dieter's nightmare."

"Is she thinking of becoming a pastry chef?"

"She doesn't know what she wants right now," he muffled through a mouth stuffed with cherry crostata. "Like a lot of kids who graduate from high school." He washed it down with a gulp of coffee. "She just knows she doesn't want to go to university and study." He paused and looked away. When he turned back to Jimmy his face had darkened. "Right now I'm sorta worried about her."

"Why's that?"

Ray glanced around, leaned forward and whispered. "A couple of days ago I got a call out of the blue from someone I hardly know. A Mrs. Moore. Told me she'd seen Gabby getting out of what she called a hot rod a couple of blocks from the restaurant, and walking the rest of the way. Like she didn't want to be seen being dropped off in front.

She gave me a description of the car but couldn't get the plate number. Said her eyesight wasn't that good."

"That's Delilah Moore. She lives across the street from us. She's a member of some committee that goes around town looking for things they think need improving."

"She was nice about it. Apologized. Said she wasn't being a busybody. Just concerned because it didn't look right to her."

"Have you said anything to Gabby?"

"No. I haven't even told Georgina yet. She would probably blow her stack and ground her. It might be something innocent. But just in case, I'm asking around about the car on the q.t. I want to know who owns it."

"Good idea."

Ray blew out a crumb-tinged breath. "You're lucky you don't have kids. Especially teenagers. Especially *girl* teenagers."

"But a guy hitting on Gabby must be a risk-taker. It's a small town. Everyone knows her dad's a cop."

"That alone scares me. Guys like that with big balls and little brains. I'm just hoping he'll see the error of his ways."

Jimmy laughed. "You sound like someone from *The Sopranos.*"

Ray sat back and laughed. "Man, wasn't that a great show? When it came on the air, I nearly crapped. I mean, how did it get past the censors?" He started singing the theme song: "Woke up this morning. Got yourself a gun. Your mama always said you'd be the chosen one."

Jimmy laughed and gestured. "Hey, Tony," he said in his best Italian accent.

Ray stopped and looked levelly at Jimmy. He spoke quietly: "If that kid lays a hand on Gabby, I might have to hurt him."

"I didn't hear that."

Nine

With Grigory handling all things legal and administrative after Irina's death, Monique took care of the personal. Through her grief, it was she who had to make the many phone calls to Irina's friends. One, in particular, had been Irina's confidant for decades. Irina had stayed in Loretta Alba's Toronto home whenever she visited the city. It was the first and most difficult conversation, but in the end, Loretta helped Monique by suggesting that she herself contact the important people in the opera world. Monique now understood why the woman had been such a stalwart friend.

Next on her list was writing the obituary. As Monique read the many articles and poured over performance programs, she was overwhelmed by her mother-in-law's amazing career. Not only had she been one of the most sought-after sopranos of her day, she was also a teacher, adjudicator, and founder and conductor of a choir.

Monique didn't know where to start, so she began by jotting down whatever came to mind. She trusted that it would eventually come together in some coherent form. After several hours of tears and cups of tea, she called Keith Kittridge and forwarded the obituary and a photograph. Next, she sketched out plans for the memorial service.

Kittridge shut his door and read the well-written words. It was a long reprise of a life well lived. He had little knowledge of the woman aside from her work in Britannia Bay and was shocked that such an eminent person had settled in such a tiny town. The picture from one of her operatic roles had probably been taken forty years before. She had been a beautiful woman, and in many ways that beauty remained into her eighties. When he had been dragged to that performance of *Messiah*, what he remembered—other than its interminable length and the *Hallelujah* Chorus—was Irina Stepanova's presence.

Then he reflected on how she had been dismissed by Diane Drake and, to a lesser extent, himself. He could feel a vein throbbing in his forehead. He picked up the copy and walked into the production room. Diane was editing an article and, intent on her work, did not notice Keith until he was beside her.

She jumped with a sudden intake of breath. "Christ! Do you always have to sneak up on me like that?" She was alert to the anger across his face.

He shoved the article at her. "Here. Read this. We should both be ashamed of ourselves." He abruptly returned to his office.

Diane skimmed through it. Then re-read it. Something about Metropolitan Opera auditions jogged her memory. She recalled sitting through one of those excruciating days years ago in Edmonton, as singer after singer sang aria after aria and being criticized to within an inch of their lives. The mind-numbing boredom resulted in her writing a scathing critique of one particularly fat soprano. Had Irina been a judge that day? She couldn't remember. She looked to see the date of the Memorial Service. She would go even if Keith didn't ask her to cover it. It was a decision she would have no time to regret.

Ten

Saturday Morning

At Graham's request, the choir had gathered to learn the information about Irina's death, the memorial service, and whether or not the scheduled performance of the Brahms *Requiem* would take place. There was whispering within the group that it seemed an ominous decision by Irina to have chosen this particular work. It took a while for everyone to quiet down as they waited for Graham to end his conversation with the rehearsal pianist.

Ariel watched him intently. He had had two days only to come to grips with Irina's death, and his loss. She thought he was doing a good job of both. But what did she know? He had been an opera singer and that required acting.

As he stepped onto the stage, he was grim-faced. "I'll get right to the major points. First of all, if there is anyone who doesn't already know this, Irina died of a massive heart attack." His voice caught. He paused, looked down briefly, then continued.

"The two things most affecting the choir right now are the performance and the memorial service. First of all, the concert will go ahead as planned; however, with different soloists. As you may have known, the original soprano and baritone had donated their services because of their friendship with Irina. They have now withdrawn."

There arose a united groan of disappointment. Someone in the tenor section shouted out, "If they were such friends, why didn't they continue as a tribute to Irina? It seems a very callous thing to do." His words were met with muttering and nods of agreement.

Graham held up his hand to silence them. "As you know, they are both busy performers. They had to squeeze in that weekend as it was. I gave them the option to cancel, and they took it. Reluctantly, I might add." The grumbling continued.

"However," and he waited until he got their attention, "we have, within our own choir, two very accomplished singers—Ariel Tan and Perry Allingham. They have agreed to take on this task."

There were gasps, then applause, and a bass bellowed out, "Well done!"

Ariel blushed. Perry, a modest man, did a good imitation of puffing up his chest, eliciting laughter and a couple of friendly thumps from his colleagues.

"Now for the memorial service. We have been asked to sing something quite unusual, and I hope we can pull it off. It's the Humming Chorus from *Madama Butterfly*. It's very difficult for the sopranos. And if you think about the scene in the opera, it's also very emotional. So, try not to watch anything on line. Just listen to it. I'm afraid there will be a lot of people who know it and will be tearing up." He paused and tried for some levity. "And I may be one of them."

There was only a bit of chuckling.

He cleared his throat. "We've printed out the music. Please work on it before next Tuesday's practice. We only have five practices before the Brahms and we have to fit in two practices of the Puccini before the memorial service in two weeks."

"Who's going to conduct us?" someone asked.

Graham smiled. "Oh, yes. A minor detail I omitted. Until we can find a permanent replacement for Irina, it will be Patricia Pullan."

They were pleased about that, as she was well known for her work in the vocal community. Even so, no one could replace their beloved Russian diva.

Eleven

Georgina was at the kitchen table quietly reading Irina's obituary in *The Bayside Bugle* when Ray breezed in from some unspecified errand. On the table was an old program from the Vancouver Opera. Ray glanced over her shoulder, then leaned around to give her a perfunctory peck on the cheek.

"What's this?" he asked absently as he shrugged out of his bomber jacket.

She held up the program, faded with age. On the cover was a stylized drawing of Cio-Cio San and Lieutenant Pinkerton embracing below blossoming cherry trees. "Do you remember this?"

Ray looked up, searching his memory bank. "God. That was so long ago. What were we? About twenty?"

"Twenty-one."

"So sue me."

"I remember because Papa bought those tickets for a kind of present after you graduated from the police academy."

"Oh yeah. That's right. We had no money then. Or now. So how come you're looking at this?"

"Take a look to see who was in it." She handed him the program.

"Irina Stepanova. Yeah, I remember that." He was about to hand it back to her.

"But check out the other name."

He frowned. "Graham Palmer. Who's Graham Palmer?"

"He's the General Manager of The Bayside Chorale. Irina's choir."

"Oh. That's a surprise."

"You think?"

"They go back a long way then." Ray shook his head. "Funny that they both wound up here. Jeez, he must be pretty broken up."

"She was married back then. And he probably was, too. He may still be, for all we know."

Ray returned the program. "I wasn't suggesting there was anything going on, Georgie. Just that they'd known each other for a long time. And here they were, still working together."

She paused. "I must have romance on my mind." Then she turned to face him. "There's something I've been meaning to tell you, but I wanted to get some information first."

"Ooh. This sounds serious. Can I fortify myself with a coffee first?" He made his way to the espresso machine. When at last he sat across from her with a large cup of cappuccino, he had to wait while she fortified herself with courage.

"There's a guy who's been sniffing around Gabby," she began. "He might be trouble."

Ray nodded. "Have you said anything to her?" He blew on his cappuccino.

"No. I wanted to check out his background before I talked to her. Or you."

He laughed. "You sound like a cop." He looked over the rim of his cup as he slurped some coffee. "Did you find out who he was?"

"I called Marcus with the description of the car. He thinks the guy

36

may be Russell Martin. They were in the same class at high school. His dad owns a car repair place out on the highway."

Ray nodded again. "Yeah. I know the shop." He continued to calmly drink his coffee.

Georgina was baffled by her husband's nonchalance. She expected him to have a little fire in his belly. "You don't seem upset."

"Why should I be? We don't know anything yet. We'll talk to Gabby and find out what's going on. If the guy's harassing her, that's one thing. But if it's something innocent, then there's no sense getting wound up about it."

"Well, I must say, I'm surprised that you're taking it in such a civilized way. I wouldn't have expected it from you—not when it comes to Gabby."

"Yeah. I'm just full of surprises." He laughed.

In fact, there *was* no need to talk to his daughter. He had just returned from a nice little chat with Russell Martin. When he had dropped hints to a few fellow officers about his concerns, Constable Tamsyn Foxcroft kept her eyes opened. On a routine patrol, she spotted Martin's car and called Ray. He told her to hold him on any pretext until he got there. When he confronted Martin, the conversation was one-sided, brief and ugly. He doubted the young man would be caught within ten miles of Gabriella from that moment on.

He was wrong.

Twelve

Toronto, Saturday evening

She is in her dressing room removing stage makeup, the whistles and cheers of the audience gradually fading in the background. It is the closing night of *Carmen*, her iconic roll. She recalls the words of one critic and repeats them aloud. "She was born for this role with her long, luxurious tresses and dark, flashing eyes. And who can ignore her zaftig body and gorgeous bosom?" A chuckle rises from the zaftig body.

Her Don Jose opens the door. "We'll save you a seat, sweetie," and blows her a kiss. The cast is gathering at its favourite watering hole. As usual after a performance, she is ravenous and hurries to finish up.

Entering the restaurant, she makes her way to the tables grouped together at the back. The cast greets her with strains from "Seguidilla." She stops them, holding out her hand and begins, "Dere's a café on de corner, run by my friend Billy Pastor. A spot where a man takes a lady when he wants to move faster. Guess I'll go and say hello to Pastor." They hoot. It's the same music, but from *Carmen Jones* — the film with Harry Belafonte and Dorothy Dandridge that she loves to this day.

The Italian owner swoons. "I change-a my name-a to Pastor-a."

Everyone is laughing. She orders. When the plate arrives, she sizes up the calorie-laden food. *There was a time when this might have killed me . . . or my career.* Now she digs in with gusto.

It had taken a mental trick to fit into her new skin. Even the reflection in the mirror did not reassure her. In her mind, she was obese, no matter proof to the contrary. It was only when she slipped into a costume transforming her into a persona—the desirable woman envisioned by a composer—that the magic happened. She then believed what she saw.

Someone says: "Have you heard about Irina Stepanova?"

Her fork falters. She holds her breath. She knows it can only be bad news. She listens, blood rushing to her ears, almost blocking out the words. She is stunned to her core. Her saviour and champion is gone.

Thirteen

March 15th

Snow, which had been "imminent" for weeks, arrived in a heart beat. It began with gently floating flakes being tossed about playfully by a whimsical wind, twisting and turning in every direction, even upwards from whence it came. Outside the Tan household, a stalwart Anna's hummingbird huddled close to the trunk of the fir tree beside the heated feeder. The sparrows, flickers, and varied thrushes were nowhere to be seen. Only a few stoic crows and stellar jays stood up to the wind and cold.

Abruptly, the atmosphere warmed and collected moisture, and in the space of a breath, the flakes transformed into huge blobs tumbling down and smothering everything in a blinding white blanket. A blink, and freezing air followed, creating a shell of ice, adding weight to the snow. Toppling trees began snapping off power lines. For several frantic days, exhausted linemen worked through the frigid cold, raising and reconnecting wires, restoring electricity to those who had survived without heat, light or well water.

After the snow melted, leaving behind slushy streets and sidewalks, the rain began—cold and relentless. This time, even the crows hid amongst the dripping branches of hundred-year old cedars. March had come in like a lion and was leaving in like manner.

It was the last rehearsal before the memorial service. Choir members dashed through the downpour toward the church entrance. Sodden jackets left large wet blotches on upholstered pews.

Patricia Pullan stepped onto the conductor's stand and waited for everyone to quiet down. Taking over the choir at this juncture was inconvenient, as she ran two others. But how could she say no?

She was small; petite, one might say. With a fresh face and pony tail, she looked to be in her twenties, but a teenage daughter altered any notion of that. She was not only similar in size to Irina but just as driven. Producing perfect performances with less than perfect singers was a challenge, but choirs had always risen to the occasion under her guidance.

Patricia was worried about the Brahms. This was her third rehearsal and the fugues were still sputtering along. She thought that after starting in January, the singers would be more proficient. But they rarely did any learning at home, expecting to polish everything at their weekly practices. At least the soloists were prepared. Tonight, though, they were going to put the final touches on the *Humming Chorus.*

"Let's get to the Puccini, shall we? Close your scores. The notes should be memorized by now." *Yeah, right,* some thought. She raised her baton, and they began. At the end, the high B strained the sopranos. Patricia stopped and showed them how to produce the sound without screeching or damaging their vocal cords. They began once more and did, more or less, what she had demonstrated.

"Well done, though I know it's a bitch to sing."

Some of them laughed. Others were not amused. They would never have heard such epithets under Madame Stepanova's watch.

Fourteen

March 19th

The morning of the memorial service began with a golden glow on the horizon that burst into glorious splendour, turning from orange to pink. Ribbons of wispy white cloud materialized as if by a magician's wand. Lit first in delicate coral, they caught fire and flamed across a crystalline sky. The spectacular display sent people rushing to photograph the sight. One scene was posted on the national weather network, irritating Newfoundlanders suffering under yet another ice storm.

Everyone had expected the church to be full but not filled. People kept scrunching together to make room for late-comers. Two rows spanning the church had been ribboned off for choir members. In front of them sat family members, and Lyudmila, who composed herself, then broke down, then composed herself, then broke down again. Her raw grief was affecting others, who had steeled themselves against being drawn into emotional displays. Now they, too, were scrabbling in their handbags and pockets for tissues.

Monique, calling on her inner reserve, stepped up to the lectern and began to deliver the eulogy.

In the foyer, a woman wearing a fashionable soft black beret with her hair tucked underneath signed the Book of Condolence, then slipped quietly inside the auditorium at the last minute. The words washed over her in waves as they ebbed and flowed with Monique's waning or waxing strength. Following her came speaker after speaker, relating what Irina had meant to them or done for them. The woman listened, all the while knowing that her own story was even more momentous. Still, their lives had been changed. Enhanced. Who was she to judge? Who knew the consequences of an action, however small? The ripple in the stream . . .

The choir had risen to the occasion and carried off the *Humming Chorus* with a level of professionalism that made everyone proud. Graham had been correct; there were sniffles when the last strains died away. An announcement was made of refreshments in the hall. People began filing out of the auditorium. Monique and Grigory were at the exit to the foyer thanking everyone and accepting words of sympathy.

Ariel, afraid of saying anything for fear of pent-up tears spilling over, gave Monique a heartfelt hug. Jimmy shook Grigory's hand and repeated the policeman's mantra, "I'm sorry for your loss," that he had said more times than he cared to remember, and which he continued to believe was almost offensively inadequate. They slowly made their way outside.

The woman with the beret stepped into the back of the line. Should she tell the Stepanovs who she was? Why she was here? She wasn't sure. Before deciding, she heard Monique's shrill voice.

"How dare you come here!" she shouted. "You were responsible for her death! How dare you!"

Shocked silence covered the crush of people. The person being verbally attacked shrank back as though physically struck.

Someone whispered, "Isn't that Diane Drake from *The Bayside Bugle*?"

"Your hateful words killed her! You're vicious. Loathsome!"

Those who were already on their way out turned back to witness the scene, blocking the doorway. Grigory took his wife's arm and turned her aside, speaking softly to her.

Diane appeared trapped and frantically looked around for another exit.

At that instant the woman saw her face and froze.

With no other way out, Diane pushed her way through the crowd and fled to her car.

The woman chased after her, all thoughts of talking to the Stepanovs forgotten. She saw Diane get into her car and speed out towards the street, close to where she was standing. She stepped back, but as it passed within a foot or two of her, she quickly peered through the windshield. *It's her. I'm sure it's her. Is that possible?* And she recalled Monique's invective. Perhaps it was.

Jimmy and Ariel, hearing the kerfuffle, had also turned back in time to see Diane pushing past mourners and running into the parking lot. When another woman ran after the reporter then try to look into Diane's car, her actions caught Jimmy's attention. Watching as she got into a car and drove off, he noted a sticker on the back bumper. "Street Fleet."

Fifteen

Edmonton, Fifteen Years Before

Nadine had made it through. It was the fifth and final required aria. As she finished her last phrase, she heard the smattering of applause. She knew her mother was out there, clapping the longest and loudest. But by this time of the day, the audience had thinned to a trickle. After all, it wasn't a concert. They hadn't had to buy tickets. And it *was* a long day. Who had the patience to sit through an entire cycle of Metropolitan Opera regional auditions? And this was only the sopranos' day. She waddled to her chair and sat, awaiting the adjudicator's feedback.

As the three judges left to confer, she sat uncomfortably on the small chair and felt her thighs seeping over the sides. At least the voluminous skirt would conceal them. She hated sitting on stage. It meant keeping your feet not more than shoulder width apart in order to maintain decorum. But she longed to spread her knees and relax. As thoughts of getting home and having a dinner dispelled some of her discomfort, the judges returned and the visiting adjudicator asked her to stand.

Her name was Irina Stepanova, a former diva who was now almost seventy. Nadine was surprised at her tiny stature, and yet she was reputed to have had incredible stamina, sustaining long phrases without losing support. Her pianissimos had left audiences on the edges of their seats. Nadine had only heard one recording of her made in the sixties.

Miss Stepanova's first words were music to Nadine's ears.

"You have a wonderful vocal instrument, Miss Portman. Lovely timbre. Perfect intonation. A silvery ring to the high notes. But I would suggest you explore the mezzo repertoire because I hear a richness in your lower register that's full of promise. It came out in your interpretation of Cherubino."

As she continued to praise her, Nadine felt faint. Her teacher told her she was very good, but she hadn't expected to hear it from a stranger, and one with such impeccable credentials.

"You need more facility with languages. For that reason, we cannot recommend that you advance at this stage, but we encourage you to continue your studies. You are young and have plenty of time. Now, you are permitted to ask questions. Is there anything you would like to know?"

"Not at the moment. Right now I can't think," she blurted out. In fact, she had several questions, but they were too personal to ask in front of others.

Irina laughed. "Well, if you do think of anything, you can get in touch with me."

"Really?"

"Yes. Your teacher has my contact information."

"Thank you."

For two days she flew about on a cloud of euphoria. Strangely, her desire for food tapered off. Then the newspaper arrived. As she read the review, Nadine felt the blood rush to her feet. She began to shake.

"Ohgod-ohgod-ohgod!" She fled as quickly to her room as her fat legs could propel her, falling on the bed and sobbing her heart out. The paper lay on the floor.

Her mother found her face down and whimpering, a pile of soggy tissues beside her. She crouched by the bed. "Nadine! Sweetheart, what's wrong? What is it?"

Nadine turned her head and looked through bloodshot eyes at her mother. "The review," she choked out and pointed to the floor.

Belle picked up the paper, read the column with rising fury, then, without another word, pulled a quilt over her daughter and went downstairs.

When Nadine's father came home from work and read the review, the look on his face frightened his wife. "That bitch. How could she do that to our little girl?" His use of profanity heightened Belle's concern, for Ellis Portman was a gentle man who seemed to dwell in a bubble of serenity. He went upstairs and gently knocked on Nadine's door. "Honey? Can I come in?"

Without hearing an answer, he opened the door and saw his daughter, his only child, hugging her Minnie Mouse doll. He came to her side. "Naddy, I'm going down to the newspaper office and I'm going do my best to get that woman fired."

Nadine started sobbing again. "I want to die."

But rather than die, she pulled herself together after three days, then called her teacher and asked for Irina Stepanova's address. She wrote, asking the questions she had wanted to ask, and included the newspaper review. It was the beginning of her transformation.

Sixteen

Britannia Bay

She barely remembered driving back to the B&B. The still, blue waters of Britannia Bay gleamed, reflecting the majestic snow-capped mountains on the mainland. But with her mind in turmoil, they might as well have been sand dunes. It had only taken a nanosecond for the pain to return. All the fame in the world could never be analgesic enough to alleviate the hurt lying in the dark recesses of her psyche.

Could it be that the same woman was here, working for some media outlet, spitting out her heartless and ignorant opinions with no regard for their effect? Or was it simply her imagination playing tricks on her? She was sure it had been Elaine Monford she had seen. But perhaps Monique shouting "poisonous words" coloured her thoughts. She had to find out more. She would make some inquiries at the B&B.

Clive Abernathy, owner of Charterhouse B&B, was busy in the entrance hall fussily arranging forsythia and pine branches into a design he assumed to be ikebana. Working away with his secateurs, he quietly hummed something tuneless; a habit when he was pleased.

He stepped back a few paces, his slightly bulging eyes blinking at his handiwork. "Maybe a bit here . . . a bit here," he said, and snipped a few tiny branches. His mouth and carefully trimmed moustache moved in pursed concentration. "Hmm. Yes."

At that moment, Calvin, their pet conure, pierced the air. While most British people exhibited a preference for dogs as pets, Clive and Daphne had fallen in love with the vividly coloured bird, although his occasional high-pitched screech had at first set their hair on end. They gradually became inured to the sound. The same couldn't be said for their guests. Fortunately, Calvin's outbursts were rare. Normally, he made small chattering noises that everyone agreed were "adorable." But he did not talk, which was fine with Clive. His wife could talk for England.

"By George, I think I've got it," he said in his plummy accent. Chuckling in satisfaction, he called out: "Daphne, do come and see my latest creation."

In the dining room, Daphne Abernathy, who often tripped over the pronunciation of her name, now came tripping into the foyer in her Mary Janes. "Oh, I say, Clive. That's brilliant!!"

"I do think I've caught that Victorian era *Japonisme,* don't you?"

Never one to find fault with her husband to his face, she agreed enthusiastically. "Oh absolutely, darling." It took so little to make him happy.

"I think I'll place that tripartite mirror behind it to reflect the three-dimensional aspect of the arrangement. What do you think?"

"Oh, quite."

A car door closing caught their attention. "I believe that will be Miss Portman." He glanced at his watch. "The memorial service must have ended. Do we have tea ready for her?"

"Yes, I'll just get the clotted cream."

"And I'll get that mirror." They disappeared, not wanting to appear as though they had been waiting for her, although, in truth, it was exactly what they had been doing. They wanted news. Gossip was manna to them.

Nadine sipped Darjeeling tea at a window table overlooking the early spring garden and stone wall decorated with espaliered fruit trees. At another time, she would have appreciated the artistry that had gone into it, but her mind was on other things.

The freshly baked scones with home-made strawberry preserves and Devonshire cream had satisfied her craving for something sweet, a Pavlovian response that happened whenever she was feeling stressed. Now she needed to satisfy her curiosity. At that moment, Daphne came in to inquire if she wanted a fresh pot of tea.

Nadine hadn't had much time to form an opinion of Daphne Abernathy and wondered if she was being too pessimistic. The woman did seem to be somewhat dense, with a penchant for breathlessly replying to the most banal questions. Nevertheless, nothing ventured. "Actually, Mrs. Abernathy—"

"Oh, please do call me Daphne, dear. We are not *that* formal here," she tittered.

Nadine smiled. "Well then, Daphne, what I need is some information and I wondered if you might help me out."

"Of course. Should I get Clive?"

Clive had been sitting in the kitchen hoping for some tid-bits of tittle-tattle. When Daphne whispered that their guest only needed some information, he made an effort to wipe the disappointment from his face.

When they returned to the dining room, Nadine observed the man in his check shirt, yellow knitted vest and bow tie. A bit portly, he nevertheless looked dapper compared to his wife, who wore . . . and she searched for a word. Frock. It looked home made and was similar in style to the one she had worn yesterday. The only difference was the pattern. Her apron matched. They stood side-by-side like sentinels, causing Nadine to straighten her own spine. She indicated the chairs. "Why don't you sit down."

"Oh. Certainly." Clive seated his wife and sat next to her.

Nadine began. "As you know, I was at the memorial service for Irina Stepanova today, and something strange and rather unsettling happened afterwards."

There was an audible intake of air from the pair.

"When we were leaving, Monique Stepanova began shouting at someone."

Daphne's hands flew up to her mouth. "Good gracious!"

"Oh, my word!" Clive struggled to contain his glee. "How utterly indecorous!"

His odd response caught her off guard. She paused. "She was accusing some woman of being responsible for Irina's death."

The pair repressed a gasp. *This was fabulous!* Daphne's pale eyes gleamed, imagining herself making this pronouncement at her book club.

"She said something about poisonous words. Do you have any idea what this could be about?"

"I might postulate a guess," Clive said. He turned to Daphne. "Do you think it could be about those music critiques, pet?"

She nodded. "Yes, yes. I'm sure that would be it."

"Right, then." He leaned forward conspiratorially. "It must have been Diane Drake she was railing at. She's the arts reporter for *The Bayside Bugle*, and writes some *particularly unpleasant* articles about local serious music groups. And those that come from elsewhere, for that matter."

"Yes, she's exceedingly rude," Daphne offered. "There have been letters to the editor."

At this, Clive got up and left the room, returning quickly with a batch of *Bayside Bugles* that he put on a sideboard. "We keep papers for our guests."

"And for Calvin's cage," Daphne added. "Not that he reads." She tittered once again.

Nadine thought Daphne resembled a bird as well, with her sharply pointed nose, jerky motions and fluttering fingers. Clive, who had been riffling through the pages of the newspaper, shot Daphne a look. "But here I am, rabbiting on," she mumbled.

"Ah, here we are," Clive said. "This one is *quite* compelling as it was Monique Stepanova's own string quartet that Diane Drake was castigating."

Nadine took the proffered paper and read the article. It was cleverly written, caustic and not very subtle. She cringed. The style was the same as Elaine Monford's. She handed the paper back to Clive. "That's awful."

"She was absolutely *beastly* when it came to *The Bayside Chorale*," Clive added. "Ms. Stepanova had been here for almost twenty years, and this *upstart* only arrived two years ago. She had no idea how hard Irina had worked to take a gaggle of amateurish singers and whip them into shape."

"Two years?" Nadine filed away the time line. "Where did she come from?"

"We don't know. All we know is that a reporter was fired one day and not long afterward, this Drake woman materialized. And with an attitude, I might add," Clive said.

"How do you mean?"

"It seemed she was bitter about something and it was reflected in her articles."

"Not all of them, Clive. She does like country and western music." They chuckled derisively.

"Does she just cover the arts scene?"

"No. She does other events as well. She actually did a rather nice write up about our Christmas lights."

"You decorate Charterhouse?"

"No." He sat taller in his chair. "I'm also *President* of Heritage Gardens. It's a *wonderful* woodland park set among the most *magnificent* old growth firs and *fabulous* rhododendrons. Every year we have an *extravagant* display of lights and holograms that cover almost the *entire* grounds. It's *quite* a draw."

At the mention of Heritage Gardens, Nadine tensed.

"It's a *marvelous* place. The tours and cream teas are *very* popular. Of course, the tours are limited now as the spring bulbs are barely up." Pausing to consider the situation, he seemed temporarily bereft. "*However*, next month we're hosting a special Easter weekend. There will be a dinner-dance on Saturday evening and an Easter Egg hunt on Sunday. Miss Drake will be covering both events."

"You could come with me tomorrow for a quick peek . . . if you could extend your visit," Daphne suggested, with hope in her voice.

"Thank you for your offer. Unfortunately, I'm unable to."

"Pity," Clive said. "It's a delightful break from worldly woes."

Nadine pondered his words. Although he had a fondness for hyperbole, in this case, his words were profound. Then Daphne spoke up, breaking the rare instance of something bordering on genuine.

"When Clive took over seven years ago, it was just a place for a walkabout. But he opened up the dining room for brunches and cream tea. And the gift shop! Well, it's simply amazing. Artisans from all over all want their crafts displayed in it. And then Clive established various events that now run throughout the year."

All Nadine heard was: *"Seven years."* She relaxed.

Clive beamed. His wife could be such an asset. "Yes, it was struggling financially. But it's now in the black and *more importantly* it's now on travel sites as a *must-see* destination."

She had a feeling they were hungry for more conversation but she was anxious to get to her room. She had things to do. "Thank you for the delicious scones and for answering my inquiry."

They jumped up simultaneously, recognizing words of conclusion, if not dismissal. "You're welcome. If you would like to take a few papers with you, please do." He motioned to the pile.

"Thank you. I'll do that." In her room, Nadine read Drake's articles. *Could* she be Elaine Monford? She needed to talk to her mother. Perhaps Belle knew when Elaine had stopped writing for *The Edmonton Times*. If it had been two years ago, then it would dovetail into her arrival in Britannia Bay. Even if that were the case, what was she doing here? And why did she change her name?

And then there was that other little surprise to share.

Downstairs, Daphne cleared away the dishes, Clive returned the papers to the library, and then they retired to the kitchen where they poured a cuppa and chatted and chortled like two mischievous children.

Seventeen

April 2nd

After word reached Keith Kittridge about the disastrous scene at the Memorial Service, his plan to have Diane preview the Brahms *Requiem* was now in tatters. What was he going to do? And what was he going to do about her? He couldn't fire her. There was an agreement. It was only a matter of time before she would be gone. In the meantime, he had to do damage control. First off, he had to ask someone with musical knowledge to write up the preview. These thoughts came to him as he skimmed the latest edition of *The Bugle*.

Edith, his wife of thirty-five years, was watching him across the breakfast table. Slim, and dressed in jeans and a pink sweatshirt, she had a youthful appearance even though her blond page-boy was now streaked with grey. She had an impish look on her face, her blue eyes twinkling. Her husband was so preoccupied looking for errors that he hadn't noticed that his half-finished plate of bacon and eggs had vanished and been replaced with a plate of sliced fruit.

As Keith put the paper aside, he looked down. "Ha ha. Very funny. You are *not* going to get me to eat fruit first thing in the morning."

"Or any other time, apparently. You *have* to eat more fruit and vegetables if you want to stay healthy."

"For the love of God, Edith. I'm not a rabbit. I've already given up cigarettes and coffee. My body is still in shock and may never recover."

"And you worry too much, too. That's not doing your heart any good."

"There's a reason I worry too much. First, the paper is on life support. I've got to find some new advertisers. And second, I've got a big problem with Diane Drake."

Edith's mouth turned down. Her brow furrowed. "I'm not surprised. She's been a thorn in your side ever since she arrived. I'm still not sure why you hired her."

He shook his head. "It's complicated. But at the time it was a godsend because I had to get rid of MacDonald. And there she was looking for a job. And she was qualified." Even though he kept few secrets from his wife, this was one he could not share with her. It was better that she not know the truth.

"Well, qualified or not, she's not a nice person."

"No, she's not. And now *The Bayside Chorale* won't let her do any more of their previews. And they have a big concert coming up in two weeks."

"Yes, I know. The *Deutsches Requiem*. Gorgeous work."

He looked at his wife with renewed interest. "You know this piece?"

"Of course. Anyone who loves choral music knows it and may even have sung it."

He went silent. His eyes headed in the general direction of her left ear; his mind gathering speed. Then he focused on her face. "Edith. I'd like to ask you something. And I'm perfectly all right with it if you say no—"

"—Which is probably a lie."

"Which it probably is." He cleared his throat. "I'm wondering—"

"Get on with it, Keith. You're only prolonging the agony."

"Right." He breathed in noisily and blew out in a sudden rush. "Would you consider doing the preview?"

Her head did a little jerk backwards as her eyes opened with surprise. "Oh, my gosh." She chewed over the idea for a couple of minutes, leaving Keith on tenterhooks.

"I'll make you a deal."

"Hmm. I have a feeling I'm going to wind up with the short straw here."

"I'll do it if you eat that fruit."

What choice did he have? Later on, he decided that it had tasted damn good, an admission that, unlike the fruit, would never pass his lips.

Eighteen

Good Friday

Ariel wasn't her normal chatty self. And she hadn't eaten her normal breakfast. Muesli meant milk, which tended to clog her pipes, and she had some serious singing to do that evening. She settled on boiled eggs, organic herbal tea and chunks of apple. Lunch was another bland meal followed by a few minutes at her steamer, breathing in warm, moist air.

Jimmy was used to her routine before dress rehearsal, so he made his own lunch and stayed out of her way, nursing a coffee and working on the cryptic crossword from a national newspaper. He had set aside *The Bugle* after reading Edith Kittridge's preview, which he thought was well written, particularly her favourable comments about the soloists.

Ariel had been pleased as well, telling Jimmy that Edith seemed to have a lot of knowledge, and that perhaps she should be doing all the classical music articles. Moreover, it would be refreshing to read something positive for once.

Then she had sequestered herself and began running through her repertoire of warmups. Finally feeling that she was ready to sing, she placed the orchestral accompaniment CD into her computer, advanced it to the appropriate place and pressed "Pause." There was only one soprano solo, but it was difficult, requiring an enormous amount of breath and support. It was marked *Langsam*. Slow. She relaxed, thought about the text, then hit "Play" and began. *Ihr habt nun Traurigkeit*. "Ye now are sorrowful."

Jimmy savoured the sounds of her sweet, clear voice. While he would be present at the performance, he felt blessed being her private audience. Well, not entirely. Roger and Molly were listening from their beds in the corner, their twitching ears the only sign that they were not truly sleeping. Just faking it.

After the music stopped, Jimmy looked up expecting Ariel to return to the kitchen. He waited, then turned back to the puzzle. But his concentration wavered between the clues and the silence in the music room. Putting aside the paper, he quietly walked down the hall and cracked open the door. Ariel was sitting, staring into space. He observed her for a minute. This was the Ariel he did not know. Everything else about her was an open book. But her communion with music was like prayer.

She turned to look at him. "Everything okay?"

He smiled. "I was going to ask you the same thing."

She nodded. "Just sitting here wondering how everything got so dumbed down."

"Sinking to the lowest common denominator, you mean?"

"Something like that. There was a time when *this* was regular everyday music," she said, lifting the score. "Now it's senseless rap. Crap is more like it. It's not music at all. Just words and rhythm." She pierced him with a familiar look.

He prepared himself for what was coming. Her rants, while filled with clear-eyed opinions, were almost an amusement for him now, although he never laughed while she was in full sail. Well, hardly ever.

"There's no quality anymore, Jimmy. Not to anything. Women dress like slags. In-your-face boobs and butts. And men with their big bellies and asses pouring out of their pants. Everything made of polyester or plastic. And no one converses anymore. They text. Their vocabularies consist of 'awesome' and 'like'." She shook her head and sighed. "Oh, I'd better put a sock in it. There's nothing I can do about it and it won't do me any good dwelling on it. It's just that sometimes I feel like I was born in the wrong century." She looked up at him with a lopsided smile. "I really should take a page out of your diary."

"It would spare you some angst."

"I'm sure it would, but I'm not going to take up Muay Thai and Judo just to get rid of my frustrations." She stood. "I think I'll go out and do some weeding. That's more my style. And it may settle my nerves."

"You don't look nervous."

"Good thing you don't have X-ray vision. You'd be shocked at all the vibrations under my skin."

"I don't know. I've been known to feel a few of your bodily vibrations from time-to-time."

She giggled.

Jimmy gave her a long hug, and began rubbing her back. "You know, Ariel, if you were born in another century, we would never have met."

"Oh, yes, we would have. We were meant to be, whatever you think. We're soulmates."

Absently continuing to knead her back, he thought about that. "Soulmate" was a word he would normally dismiss, as it had become a cliché. But it was true. They did complete each other.

Her muffled voice came from somewhere near his armpit. "That feels wonderful."

"At your service. You know it's drizzling out there, don't you?"

"It'll make weeding that much easier." She broke away. "Have you finished the cryptic?"

"Almost done."

"Did you make a blank copy for me?"

"Of course. Do I not value my life?"

"Okay. I'll go outside, then I'll come in and do the puzzle. That should get me through the rest of the day."

Jimmy looked at her slyly. "Maybe."

"What do you mean?"

"It may take you more than a day to finish it."

She narrowed her eyes. "Is that a challenge, Adorable Ass?"

He laughed. "No. It's a heads-up, Spunky Lady."

"Well, we shall see about that. The weeding can wait."

Nineteen

Saturday

Even though they were said half in jest, Kittridge's parting words to Diane raised her hackles. "You have to cover that Easter Egg Hunt tomorrow morning, so don't enjoy yourself too much tonight."

As if, she thought. A dinner dance and raffle was not her idea of a thrilling night out; a raffle for a chance to smash a piñata and claim what was inside. It was supposed to be a free ten-day trip somewhere. *Duh! Piñata. Mexico, anyone?* But at least she had been spared the agony of previewing the concert. Kittridge's wife had done a better job than she ever could have done. She hoped it would be a permanent arrangement leaving her to cover events and other music—music she liked. Kittridge hadn't yet clued her in.

There was just time enough to have a bite to eat, change into something more appropriate and get to the venue. Heritage Gardens had begun hosting more special occasions in addition to their regular lunches and cream teas. And, according to the bush telegraph, they were managing to snag some of the golfers away from the Nineteenth Hole, which wasn't going down too well with the owners of the golf course. At least the Gardens wasn't planning to offer dinners. There were few residents in the village willing to open their wallets for a restaurant meal more than a couple of nights a week. And Catalani's was usually their first choice.

Diane's own paycheque and palate tended toward takeaway, which she would eat while trolling the web or working. It wasn't much of an existence, but she didn't want to be out there taking any risks. She had stopped that after the last incident when she had had one too many drinks. Being as low-profile as possible would continue to be her life for a while. She sighed, thinking again what a comedown this was. But at least she was safe in Britannia Bay.

She rifled in the back of the closet looking for her only winter suit. It had been her staple for many years. With a white wool turtleneck sweater, the calf-length black suit and leather boots were just the right statement of *bon chic, bon genre*. In a way, she welcomed tonight's gig. It gave her a chance to dress up and pretend to be just another guest. But her big black holdall containing her camera, iPad, work cellphone, and handbag would squelch any ideas of blending in.

The Civic Centre was jammed to the rafters, almost literally, as risers had been added to the back of the vast room in order to accommodate everyone. Publicity posters and Edith Kittridge's preview had done the job. An augmented orchestra, with several musicians from out of town, required choir members to billet as many as they could manage for three days. The tympanist had travelled up from Victoria in his RV, his cumbersome instruments and beloved chocolate lab taking up most of the room inside. But at least he had his own space and familiar company. Clive and Daphne Abernathy were delighted that their B&B was fully booked, something that rarely happened in April.

The program was printed in German and English, as the text was essential to understanding the music—the alternate drama and lyricism, the sweeping, soaring melodic lines and fast and furious fugues. A quick read imparted the meaning and allowed the audience to be drawn in. Many came expecting it to be a religious work, and were surprised to learn that it was a secular humanist work.

Jimmy had not discussed the *Requiem* with Ariel, and appreciated the program notes. When the music began, he knew in his bones that he would be experiencing one of the greatest choral works of all time. After the beautiful Fourth Movement that some people recognized as, "How Lovely is Thy Dwelling Place," Patricia paused for a few moments.

It was now Ariel's moment to shine. The choir would remain sitting while singing their soft phrases during her solo. She stood and almost floated toward centre stage in her stunning gown of shimmering blue silk. She had been told: "No black," and she was happy to oblige. Patricia turned and gave her big eyeballs and a small grin. Then she gave the downbeat.

Jimmy's heart swelled with pride. He had fallen deeply and stupidly in love with Ariel from the moment they first spoke. They had been sitting opposite each other during the first day of history class. Looking back on it, he wondered what it was about her that had caught his attention. Was it her pretty face and inquisitive blue eyes, or was it the intelligence in her remarks? Or was it perhaps her lingering glances at him? After class, he waited for her. They fell in step with the briefest of words, and had walked together ever since. And look where the road had taken them.

Ariel began the phrase he had heard hundreds of times. But here, with the orchestra and the audience, it was so much more. There was an energy in the room that enhanced every line. He was caught up in it and found himself holding his breath. It was magical.

As she packed away her equipment, Diane admitted that the evening hadn't been that bad. The *piñata* was a clever way to extend the excitement of the raffle. The winner, a petite woman, had tried time and again to smash the colourful burro, creating increasing laughter with each attempt. Finally, a man hoisted her up and she managed to break it open. When she pulled out the envelope announcing the trip to Mexico, everyone cheered. Diane had her breathless interview on tape and a good group photograph for the paper. That always made readers happy, she thought, as she made her way to the exit and to a waiting golf cart that would take her at least as far as the parking lot. From there, it was only a short walk to her car, which was parked on the street due to the overflow.

"I'm sorry, Miss Drake," the doorman said, as she stepped outside. "The driver has just left. He won't be back for about twenty minutes. Unfortunately, there's only one vehicle tonight."

"Darn!" Her mood soured. Not having taken advantage of the buffet food, she was hungry. And now only the bar was open. She needed sustenance and wanted to write up her report while it was fresh in her mind.

Fog had drifted in—a dense, cold and wet blanket—damp enough to seep into clothing. She stepped back inside to wait. But waiting for anything was not part of her make-up.

"I'm going to walk," she informed him, after a few frustrating minutes.

"Are you sure you want to do that? It's a bit of a hike. And the weather is decidedly uncooperative."

"I know, but the exercise will do me good. Good night." She hefted the heavy bag over her shoulder. bade him good night and began hoofing it up to Bayside Drive. The opacity intensified the darkness, but at least there were intermittent lights embedded in the ground alongside the road. With the heels of her boots clacking on the pavement and her loud panting, she did not heard the footsteps behind her.

"Diane."

Surprised, she turned around. She could make out the shape of someone, but with only the faint glow from the lights, she couldn't tell if it was a man or a woman. The voice was muffled.

"Hello. Who is it?"

"Or should I say, Elaine?"

She froze, then dropped her bag and turned to run, but too late. A hand gripped her arm, jerking her back around. A punch landed on her jaw. She gasped, staggered backwards, and slammed her head on the pavement. Sharp pains shot through her body. Jagged light flashed underneath her eyelids. She felt her shoulders being lifted and her limp body bumping across soft, soggy earth. *Oh, God! He's going to kill me!* It was her last thought before everything went black.

The applause and bravos continued for several minutes. When it finally died down and the choir and orchestra made their way to the respective "green rooms," Jimmy waited in the foyer, listening to the rapturous praise as people left the building. He wanted to shout: "My wife was the soloist!" Instead, he stood silently aside and smiled.

With Delilah clutching Lana's arm, the pair came up to him, their faces beaming. "That wife of yours knocked my socks off, Jimmy. I had no idea she could sing like that. It was beautiful!"

"Sure wasn't like us scattin' in the kitchen," Lana said, laughing.

"I didn't know what to expect," Delilah said. "I was afraid I would fall asleep—you know, being classical music and all. But it was pretty exciting." She yawned.

"Speaking of sleep, time to get you home, Delilah." Lana gave Jimmy a hug. "Tell Ariel how thrilled we were."

"I will. Thanks for coming."

Most of the audience was long gone by the time the performers began trickling out. Ariel soon followed with several choir members.

They were high on adrenalin and joy. Some knew Jimmy.

"Wasn't she wonderful?"

"Wasn't it a fabulous performance!"

"I'll bet you're proud of her."

He kept nodding and saying, "Yes" and sidled towards Ariel.

Before he could hug her, she grabbed his arm. "C'mon. Let's get out of here!"

"What? No public displays of affection?"

She laughed. "I'm starving. A bunch of us are going to Catalani's."

The food and wine kept spirits going until long after the kitchen closed. In order to get rid of her customers, Georgina finally began turning off the lights.

"What a day!" Ariel said, when they got home. After slipping off her gown, removing her makeup and washing her face, she fell into bed, exhausted. Jimmy and the cats joined her. He was looking forward to a long lie-in the following morning.

Twenty

Easter Sunday

A sliver of milky light pierces the slate grey clouds. Fingers of fog cling to tree tops. The taste of salt tang wafts in from the bay. An old raccoon hobbles its way down toward the manor—and food.

Soggy ground silences the man's footsteps. Puffs of air float away with each breath. The damp bothers his bones. Spotting a patch of bright blue, he kneels to push away a bit of mouldering leaf from the scilla. Here and there, miniature daffodils crowd together in clumps. They are late in this deep, dark wood. The sight of purple woodland violets shooting up through the loamy soil fills him with inexplicable joy.

He is alone; bird songs his only company. A short-lived shower has fallen overnight but not enough to create puddles or spoil the day. He lifts three decorated eggs from his basket and carefully places them under a hellebore. Soon the shrieks and laughter of little children will fill the air as they search for treasures of coloured Easter eggs hidden beneath the shrubs.

~ ~ ~

The Board of Heritage Gardens had protested that children would not stick to designated areas and would trample over the flower beds. But Clive Abernathy had dug in his heels. He argued that there had to be more events to bring in money. It was a monumental task trying to preserve a valued garden and woodland, notwithstanding a generous stipend from the Town Council. And then there were the plans for a proper parking lot. As things stood, the current one was not adequate and the overflow wound up on Bayside Drive. A former highway, it was a dangerous alternative. Even though the speed limit had been lowered to match that of the city, drivers still treated it like a turnpike.

Thus, the dinner dance and raffle, and the Easter Egg hunt. Abernathy was praying that parents would remain afterwards and take advantage of the dining room and gift shop. Extra staff had been hired for the occasion, and the President of Heritage Gardens Society would be vigilantly watching the bottom line.

~ ~ ~

Turning off the road and onto the grass, he notices that the manicured lawn has been disturbed. *Hudiča! Jelen.* He grabs his rake, intending to repair deer tracks, but quickly realizes the damage was not caused by deer. Puzzled, he walks along the flattened grass and comes upon a narrow, shallow channel carved in the dirt. He looks up to where it ends—under a low, heavy cedar bough. He is struck by a feeling of dread. Creeping closer, he takes his rake and lifts the bough. The boots are what he sees first. And then . . . *Drek! Drek*! He drops the rake, runs back to the road, gropes in his vest pocket for his phone—then vomits.

The trilling of Jimmy's cellphone nudged him out of his slumber. *So much for sleeping in,* he thought. He saw the caller ID and quickly picked up. "I'm here, Ray." He looked at the time. 6:45.

"And I'm about five minutes from your house, so I hope you're up and dressed. We've got a body. And it's no accident."

Jimmy jumped up heading for the bathroom, sending Roger tumbling over Molly, who batted him with her paw and hissed. The movements woke Ariel. "What the heck?" she uttered, removing her eye mask. She saw two cats facing off, tails twitching, and an empty space where her husband should have been. She got out of bed.

Jimmy hurried back to the bedroom. Without a word, he threaded his legs into his pants. While he fumbled with the zipper, Ariel, alert to what was happening, retrieved a shirt and held it open for him. He fit his arms through the sleeves and stood silent as Ariel deftly fastened the buttons. His eyes were grave when they met hers. She knew that look and felt the familiar wave of nausea welling up, certain that there had been a suspicious death. It was the only thing that could have him rushing around in a state of controlled panic.

Hurrying to the cupboard where he kept his special gear, he tugged on his boots and grabbed his padded jacket and duty belt. Ariel opened the door for him. He gave her a quick kiss, ran out to where Ray was waiting and disappeared inside the vehicle.

"So, I'll see you when I see you," Ariel said quietly to the receding van, her heart thumping in her chest.

It wasn't difficult to spot the crime scene venue. The area around Heritage Gardens was vibrant with colour. Orange cones sealed off one lane of traffic on Bayside Drive. Flashing red, white and blue lights on police cars pulsated rhythmically. Yellow police tape fluttered across the service entrance road. Constables Adam Berry and Simon Rhys-Jones were directing traffic that had doubled in the past half hour. It hadn't taken long for news of a police incident to hit the phone lines. A small group of looky-loos had soon gathered about, gawking.

Constable Craig Carpenter, a.k.a. The Incredible Hulk, shooed away the curious who ventured too close, and lifted the tape for official cars. He was also responsible for the Crime Scene Entry Log. Ray paused while Carpenter took down their badge numbers and the time.

"You'll have to walk down."

"Why's that?" Ray asked.

"The MCV is down there blocking the road. Only the golf carts are able to get through."

Ray looked at Jimmy, who shrugged. "I'm okay to walk."

"How far is it?" Ray asked. "I can't see anything from here except trees."

"It's beyond the bend in the road. It'll take a good ten minutes."

Jimmy watched Ray weighing the options. "You need the exercise," he said.

"Hey! Watch your mouth!"

They heard the loud thrumming of the MCV's generator before they saw the vehicle. It reminded Ray of the old DC-3 engines that had always put him to sleep soon after take-off. Under the careful guidance of Constable Mike Heppner, it had lumbered down the narrow road and come to a halt near the crime scene. Now the officially designated operator, Heppner powered up the sixteen-foot mast containing four bright LED lights creating an other-worldly contrast to the dim, natural light.

Scene-of-Crime-Officer John Atkins was grateful for the vehicle's illumination as he carefully measured and sketched the scene. Several tree branches had been tethered away from the body, now protected from the elements by a modified crime scene tent. Three other SOCOs were diligently at work. Gene McDaniel was in the process of photographing the body. Dalbir Dhillon was bagging and tagging, fingerprinting and swabbing, while Tim Novak was searching the grounds for the victim's belongings.

Ray and Jimmy stepped into the MCV. "Hey, Mike," Ray said. "How was it driving this beast down this road?"

"Wobbly. Had to fight it."

"But you're grinning," Jimmy said as he donned his forensic gear.

"What can I say? Every boy likes a big, noisy truck."

Suited up in their PPE, the two detectives ducked into the tent. Even through the pallor of death, the victim showed signs of beauty. "Not a bad-looking woman," Ray said softly and clicked his tongue. He squatted to get a closer look at her face. "Isn't her jaw out of alignment?" he asked no one in particular. "She didn't get that from falling on the pavement. Someone socked her," Ray said.

There were nods from the others.

He examined her apparel. The black wool coat and skirt were matted with mud and garden debris. They were of good quality, as were her leather boots and gloves. Everything was on the expensive side. He got up and motioned to Jimmy. They exited, leaving McDaniel and Dhillon to their tasks.

Tamsyn Foxcroft stood at the entrance to the tent. "Who found her?" Ray asked.

She looked at her clipboard. "Pavel Horvath. He's one of the gardeners."

"Where is he now?"

"Inside the house."

"Were you able to bag his clothes?"

"Yeah." Her nose wrinkled. "They were covered in puke. Thank God he had street clothes in his locker."

"Has anyone questioned him yet?"

"No. That's your job."

Ray and Jimmy laughed at her cheek.

"I'll go and talk to him," Jimmy said. He turned to Ray. "This is your fault, you know," he said under his breath.

Ray started. "How do you figure that?"

"You tempted Fate." He jabbed him on the arm then walked off.

"Oh, yeah. Right. I'm so all powerful," he called after him before turning back to Tamsyn.

"What was all that about?" she asked.

He shook his head. "Nothing. Just something I said. Anyway, what was the gardener doing here so early?"

"He was putting out tape to block off areas for the Easter Egg hunt," she said. "A lot of kids are going be disappointed."

Novak walked over to them.

"Do we know who she is?" Ray asked him.

"No. If she had a handbag, we haven't found it yet. And there was nothing in her pockets."

"Has anyone called the M.E.?"

"I did," Novak replied. "She said she'd be here in a half an hour. That was about fifteen minutes ago."

Ray returned to the site of the attack. The dark stain of blood on the pavement had been identified with a marker. Hearing a quiet whining noise, he looked up to see Chief William Wyatt coming down the road in a golf cart with Dr. Dayani Nayagam by his side. *That will put him in a good mood,* Ray thought.

The driver stopped and the Medical Examiner alighted daintily carrying her crime scene bag. "Hello, detective," she greeted him with a smile, showing dazzling white teeth against her tawny skin. This morning her curves were covered with a Burberry trench coat, her feet shod in Flinton boots.

"Good morning, Dr. D. Good morning, Chief."

Wyatt grabbed the side rail and hauled himself out, after which the driver made his way back up the road.

Wyatt grunted. "Not so good. What have we got?"

"White female. Maybe late thirties, early forties. Attacked right where I'm standing. Dressed nice. So probably at the dance last night. Body dragged about thirty yards. Left under a cedar tree." He gestured in the general direction. "No ID yet."

"Any signs of a sexual assault?"

"Doesn't appear to be. Her jaw looks broken, though."

Dr. Nayagam nodded towards the MCV. "That's going to make things faster and easier."

Wyatt's achievement got the better of him. "We're the envy of stations all over the island," he boasted.

"Congratulations." A twinkle in her eye slipped out before she could catch it. "Well, I'd better get to it."

Ray watched Wyatt watching her. He knew the man was happily married, but his fascination with the Medical Examiner was teenage crush time.

Wyatt turned to Ray. "What do you think, Rossini?"

I think you're a damn fool, he wanted to say. "Possible fouled-up robbery."

"Oddly enough, there was opportunity for it. I talked to the golf cart driver. He said there was a snafu last night. One of the carts was out of commission. Who knows? It might have a bearing on the case."

"Hmm. Okay. After Jimmy finishes interviewing the gardener we'll have a talk with him."

"He's gone back up to the parking lot to wait for Abernathy, the manager." Wyatt entered the MCV and reached for a bundle of protective gear. "There's someone in the maintenance shed repairing the other cart. He might know something." He tugged on the overalls, then leaned down to put the booties over his shoes, grunting as he did so. "Go talk to him after we observe Dr. D. at work."

It was the last thing Ray wanted to do. Hot chocolate was on the menu and he needed to pee. "I'll catch up with you," he said, knowing his priorities.

So far, Jimmy's attempts to pry information from Pavel Horvath were like trying to milk a monkey. The man was shaking. Anxiety deepened the criss-crossed lines of a face that in normal circumstances would have been the colour of a walnut shell. Right now it was more like grey chalk. The faint smell of vomit lingered around him. As he attempted to answer one of Jimmy's questions, he faltered and put his hand over his mouth swallowing quickly a few times.

"Would you like a glass of water?" Jimmy asked him.

He shook his head.

Striking out with the standard questions, Jimmy decided to ask him where he was from. The change in the man was dramatic. As he spoke of Slovenia, his body relaxed. His face became animated as he described the scenery and the food and the attractions in Bled, his home town.

Jimmy had to ask exactly where it was because small Eastern European countries kept changing names and allegiances in the 20th century. He learned that it was snug against Italy on the Adriatic and had been part of Yugoslavia until 1991. It was also Melania Trump's birth country.

"That must have raised the country's profile," Jimmy said.

Horvath smiled briefly. "She is beautiful. Like all Slovenian women."

Jimmy made no comment, allowing an interval to elapse. He needed to return to the matter at hand. "Mr. Horvath, can you think of anything else that might help us?"

"No. I ran as soon as I saw . . ." His words trailed off.

Jimmy removed one of his cards and handed it to him. "If you think of anything, no matter how small, call me. Quite often the initial shock clouds a person's mind and then later he or she remembers something that seems insignificant, but turns out to be important."

Horvath listened with interest to this information. He hoped that it would happen to him. He would like to feel important.

Jimmy changed tack again. "If I might ask, what brought you to Canada, since Slovenia is such a nice place?"

"My son is enrolled at the Bamfield Marine Sciences Centre. He is doing graduate work in marine biology. We wanted to be near him. I needed to work. This was closest."

Jimmy heard the pride in his voice. Then he wondered about the man's working visa, but quickly put that out of his mind. It was not his concern. After all, his own background wouldn't bear close scrutiny.

Twenty-one

When Ray stepped through the front door and onto a highly polished parquet floor partially covered by a Persian rug, he felt as though he were walking into the top floor of *Upstairs Downstairs*. The room was overstuffed with antiques—tapestry-upholstered chairs and love seats, small occasional tables, bric-a-brac and paintings. Colourful scenes of country gardens graced the wallpaper. There were even the stereotypical aspidistras in two large brass urns. He had no idea when the edifice was built, but guessed that it would have been in the early 1900s. He felt some embarrassment at never having visited the historical attraction. *When this case is over, I'll bring Georgie.*

Hearing voices, he headed in their direction. Jimmy was in what Ray judged to be the original library, but only a small section of shelving remained for books. The room was now a gallery of paintings and photographs of the manor from its earliest days to its transformation as a tourist destination.

Jimmy had wrapped up his questioning of the gardener, who passed by Ray with a soft, "Excuse me." Waiting until the man was out of earshot, Ray turned to Jimmy. "What's the skinny?"

"He doesn't remember much right now. He said he didn't notice any details. Just ran away and called 9-1-1. He's pretty rattled."

"One of the golf carts was out of commission last night, so people had to wait. They weren't about to walk up to the parking lot in the dark. But it looks like our victim decided to do just that. There's a maintenance worker here. Let's go chat him up. See if he knows anything."

A six-seater cart with a striped green and white canopy was sitting without its bank of batteries, which were resting on a workbench. A man dressed in overalls hovered over them. Noticing their entrance, he put down his tools and walked toward them, wiping his hands on a shop cloth that bore the stains of oil and grease.

"Hello, gentlemen. What can I do for you?" Thankfully for them, he didn't offer to shake hands.

Ray introduced himself and Jimmy as police officers and asked for his name.

"Charlie Ulrich," and spelled it out when he noticed Jimmy ready with a small notebook and pen.

Ray pointed to the gutted golf cart. "I'm assuming this is the cart that wasn't available last night."

The man nodded. "Yep."

Ray gave Jimmy a look that said *I'll take this.* "So you only had the one? That must have been inconvenient."

"It was more than inconvenient. It made us look like a bunch of yokels," he said with disgust.

"Are you one of the drivers?"

"No. I'm the mechanic."

"Do you do all the mechanical work here, Mr. Ulrich?"

"Pretty much. You could say I'm Abernathy's dogsbody." He indicated various power tools and machines used to maintain the garden. "I keep all of them running, which is a full-time job in itself. Some are pretty old, but Abernathy won't shell out for new ones."

Ray sized up the man. He would have been one of those hard-working manual labourers proud of his skills. Perhaps a retiree, by his age, but still wanting to work rather than sit around playing cards with his cronies at the seniors' centre.

"How many drivers are there?"

"Jack, the man on duty right now, and Ralph Tucker."

"So who remained on duty last night?"

"Tucker. Abernathy sent Jack home when his cart went tits up."

"What time does Tucker's shift start?"

"Well, there aren't any regular shifts right now. Heritage Gardens is only open on Sundays for brunch and afternoon tea. We only need one driver, and that would be Tucker. But since he stayed late last night, Jack came in." He glanced at a large wall clock. "Tucker's probably still in bed."

"Can you tell us anything about what happened last night?"

"No. I was at emergency. My wife fell and broke her wrist. When I got home from the hospital there was a message on my answering machine that one of the carts was not operational. Abernathy needed me to come in and fix it first thing today. Derek Bishop is the man you'll want to talk to. He was the doorman on duty. He'll have more information."

"Do you have the phone numbers for these men?"

"I have Tucker's. Don't know about Bishop's. I'll look." In the corner of the room stood a beat-up wooden desk. Pushing around papers and manuals, Ulrich brought out an old-fashioned rolodex. He found both numbers and gave them to Ray, saying: "Today's Easter Egg Hunt was supposed to be a cash cow event for a new parking lot." His lips twisted into a wicked grin. "*President* Abernathy is going to be smokin' hot."

Ulrich's comment perfectly reflected Clive Abernathy's current state. Being kept in check near the MCV, he was sizzling like grilled bacon, his face red, eyes nearly popping out of his head. He railed at Chief Wyatt. "This is an *utter* and *complete catastrophe!*" The Easter Egg Hunt that was supposed to start in—" he looked at his watch—"two and a half hours. And now the day is *ruined!*" He watched as the crime team moved about. "And look how they're tramping down the *shrubbery* and mucking up the *grounds*. Do they have to behave like a herd of *elephants*?"

Making their way back to the MCV, Ray and Jimmy heard the last of the rant. Ulrich's mocking of Abernathy's title became clear. No doubt he saw him as a pompous buffoon. Even at this early morning hour he was a dressed in waxed jacket, tweeds, flat cap and brogues.

"Mr. Abernathy?" Ray stepped in, hoping to put a lid on the man's rising anger. "I'm Detective Sergeant Rossini and this is D.S. Tan. We need to ask you some questions about last night."

Abernathy, oblivious to Ray's request, carried on. "How soon will you be out of here so that I can open the Gardens? I need to salvage *some* part of the day. We've got staff arriving. Eggs still have to be put out." He looked up thinking of all the things that had to be done.

"Mr. Abernathy," Wyatt interrupted, voice firm. "This is a crime scene."

Abernathy suddenly snapped to attention and gawped at him. "*A crime?* I thought it was just an *accident* of some kind." He paused. "Oh, good God. How *awful*. That means I'll have to cancel the event." His mind took off on a tangent. "I must notify the staff. And there should be some kind of public announcement."

"The press is already up there," Wyatt's chin motioned toward Bayside Drive. "No doubt the radio station has already broadcast the news. Now, would you please accompany the detectives inside so that they can ask you some questions."

Abernathy, deflated and defeated, nodded and led the detectives back into the manor.

Wyatt turned to Mike Heppner. "Boy, he's a royal pain in the ass, isn't he?"

"Couldn't have said it better myself, Chief."

Abernathy noticed how quiet it was inside. Normally the kitchen staff would be preparing menu items. He walked through to the library and removed his jacket and cap, which left strands of his comb-over sticking out from his scalp. All the air had escaped his puffed-up chest. He slumped in a wingback chair on one side of the gas-lit fireplace and buried his face in his hands.

Jimmy sat across from him and Ray took the loveseat. "The first thing we need is your guest list from last night—names, addresses and phone numbers," Ray said.

Abernathy looked up and nodded. "It's on the computer in the office. Shall I print it out?"

"If you wouldn't mind."

He slowly rose and, with drooping head, slouched out of the room. Ray whispered: "I wonder if there's a surveillance camera located anywhere near the front door."

Jimmy got up and left the room to check. He returned, shaking his head. "There doesn't seem to be any kind of camera. But there has to be some alarm system."

"It would help if we could see when the vic left. And if she was alone."

A phone rang in the distance. They heard part of a recorded message that was immediately stopped. Then they heard: "Regret . . . emergency situation . . . cancelled." Abernathy returned with a two-page print out. He put it into Jimmy's outstretched hand. "People are calling wanting to know what is happening." His tone was flat.

"Do you have a video of the event last night?"

"Yes. We had a staff photographer taking videos and stills during the evening, especially when the raffle was taking place. I'm sure most attendees remained until the winner was announced and the *piñata* was broken."

"What time was that?"

"About 9:30."

"Do you know if those images are on your computer?"

"I'm sure he uploaded them before he left."

"We'd like to take a look at them, if you don't mind."

Ray and Jimmy suppressed their excitement. Things were rapidly moving along toward discovering the victim's identity.

"What do you want to see first, the video or the photographs?"

"The photographs," Ray said.

They followed him to his office where Abernathy opened the appropriate folder and slowly scrolled through the photographs.

After several minutes, something caught Jimmy's attention. "Who is that?" He pointed to a lone female in the background, her face obscured by the camera she was holding up. But he could see a white top under a black suit.

Abernathy peered at the screen. "That's the person from the press. She's going to do a write up and put a group picture and a picture of the raffle winner in *The Bayside Bugle*."

"Are you referring to Diane Drake?" Jimmy asked.

"Yes." He made a tiny moue with his mouth and quietly added: "The infamous Diane Drake."

Ray looked at Jimmy with raised eyebrows.

"Do you know if she stayed after she took those photographs?"

"I really couldn't tell you. But Derek might be able to help in that regard. He's the doorman." It seemed to Jimmy that Derek was the man of the hour.

Keith Kittridge was tying a knot in his tie. Being in the choir, Edith had already left for church. Easter Sunday was his biannual religious duty—the other being Christmas. And if it hadn't been for his wife, he would have put a pass on both occasions. He couldn't stand being a captive audience unless he actually *was* captivated by a particularly riveting performance of some kind.

He was making for the door when his cellphone rang. The screen showed his news reporter's name. "Morning Nate. What's up?"

"There's something serious going on at Heritage Gardens, Keith. I'm on the road opposite the entrance. It's blocked off with police cars and a humongous police vehicle is down there and an ambulance just left."

"Okay. Sounds like a story. Do your best to get a statement from the police," he said with resignation. His experience with the boys in blue was not the best. It was the old antagonism between the police and the press. Getting information from them was like extracting impacted molars.

He shut off his phone and regretfully left for church. A hot news story and there he would be warming his tuchus on a pew.

Twenty-two

Returning to the CVU with their information, Jimmy called a sleeping Ralph Tucker and told him to come to the Gardens immediately. Next he called Derek Bishop and politely requested him to meet them in the library of the manor. Bishop said he had heard the news and was expecting their call. He would be down directly. Then Jimmy instructed Carpenter to let both men through the tape.

Dr. Dayani had already left. The body had been taken to the hospital morgue. McDaniel was busy transferring his photographs to the computer and opening them onto the two monitors.

"We think we have the identity of the victim, Chief," Ray said to Wyatt, who was sipping coffee from the unit's Keurig machine.

"Who is it?" He looked up expectantly.

"From what Abernathy told us, we think it's Diane Drake from *The Bayside Bugle*. She was here taking shots of the party for the paper. The doorman will most likely know when she left. He should be here shortly. And the driver on duty last night is on his way as well."

"Diane Drake, eh?" He pointed to the computer screen. "Gene, could you print out a copy of one of those photos? We need to have something to show the doorman."

"Do you want me to photoshop one, make her look less . . . uh . . . dead?" McDaniel asked.

Wyatt grimaced. "Might be a good idea."

Derek Bishop had the serene air of an English country gentleman. Lounging comfortably on the loveseat, he exuded confidence and dignity. Jimmy pictured him as someone who could easily have been the owner of the manor. Wearing wide-wale corduroys, heavy walking shoes and a parka with multiple pockets, he was tall and slim. And very erect. Somewhere in his seventies, he still had an abundance of white hair and a neatly trimmed beard. His grey eyes were alert, although one appeared to be slightly off-centre. He smelled faintly of limes.

After introductions were made, Ray asked him to recall what time Diane Drake left. Bishop looked sharply at him. "Is that the deceased?" When Ray affirmed that it was, Bishop shook his head. 'Oh, dear." He extracted a cellphone from his jacket pocket. "I keep a log. We had a list of the attendees and I checked them in and out."

Ray glanced over at Jimmy. His look suggested that things were getting better and better.

"Ah, yes, here we are," Derek said. "I have her checked out at 10:00. But she didn't leave then. I told her that the driver had just left with a group of guests and most likely would not return for about twenty minutes. I suggested she stay inside out of the damp until he returned. She was rather impatient. After about ten minutes, she said she didn't want to wait any longer, that she had work to do, and started off on foot. I tried to dissuade her, but she was having none of it. It's at least a fifteen-minute hike up to the highway. The heels on her boots were high, and that in itself would make the trek more arduous. Frankly, I thought she was a bit mad."

Ray pulled out the photograph. "Is this the woman?" He handed it to Bishop, who removed a pair of half-rim glasses from a hard-shell case. At first, he drew back at the sight of the body. "Oh, heavens." Then he looked more closely at McDaniel's enhanced shot. He sighed and handed it back to Ray. "Yes, that is Miss Drake."

"Did most people stay for the entire evening?"

"No. As a matter of fact, a small group left just after the raffle. and before dessert and coffee."

"Was that when the driver returned late from one of his rounds?"

Bishop gave a slight nod. "Yes. He should have returned in time for the 9:30 run. But he was about ten minutes late and it backed up every other trip. It wasn't a major inconvenience. It's just that we like to run a tight ship here." He smiled.

"Thank you. You've been very helpful," Ray said.

"I'll take my leave then, detectives."

He walked out, his stance a little less erect.

"He seems a fine man," Ray observed.

"Looks like he attended a military school or was even in the military."

"Maybe the navy. You know—his reference to a tight ship."

Seconds later, a breathless and nervous Ralph Tucker rushed into the manor. The contrast to Derek Bishop was despairingly clear. With uncombed hair, blood-shot eyes and a five-o'clock shadow, Tucker was mildly repugnant. His clothes were rumpled and reeked of cigarette smoke. As if to emphasize his habit, he broke out into hacking coughs filled with phlegm and tar. Jimmy nearly gagged along with him.

Ray was similarly disgusted. "Take a seat," he said sharply, and began with a few preliminary questions before getting to the heart of the inquiry. "What we want to know is why you were late returning on one of your runs last night."

~ ~ ~

The guests were cramming into the cart, the women laughing as they pretended they would have to sit on someone's knee. Tucker helped in one chunky woman who had had one too many. She giggled. "Sorry. I seem to be a bit off balance."

"Unbalanced is more like it," said one, which got them chortling.

Tucker clenched his jaw. He had to pee and had no time to run back to the maintenance shed. There was only one thing he could do. Driving the cart as fast as it would go, he waited in the parking lot until the passengers got to their cars, then ran behind a large tree. While relieving himself, he heard a rattling metal noise. It sounded like someone was climbing up the service gate. Fastening his fly, he returned to the cart, picked up his Maglite and crept a few feet toward the gate. He shone the beam around but didn't see anything. *I'll be damned if I'm gonna go after anyone trying to get in. Abernathy don't pay me enough to do that. Maybe I should just radio Bishop.* He thought about that, then decided to do nothing. It would only mean a hassle. Pulling out a pack of cigarettes, he lit one and drew in the smoke. He began to feel human again.

~ ~ ~

Tucker gulped, sending his prominent Adam's apple bobbing up and down his thin neck as he offered his explanation.

"So how long did this take you?" Ray asked.

"I dunno. Maybe ten minutes."

"Ten minutes to take a pee and check the gate?"

He cleared his throat. "Well . . . uh . . . I had a smoke, too. We're not allowed to smoke in the cart. Or anywhere. So, I usually grab a fag when I'm up top."

"So what time was this, when you heard the sound?" Ray and Jimmy already had an approximate time, but Ray wanted Tucker to stew a little.

"Uh . . . um . . . I'm not sure exactly." His right knee began to jerk up and down like a jackhammer.

"Well, was it early in the evening or later on?"

"Oh. Ah. It was early. Right after the dinner but before the raffle. It was my first trip."

"Okay. So that was around 9:15 or so."

Tucker shrugged. "I guess so."

"And you didn't see anything suspicious on the road during any of your trips?"

"Like what?"

Ray nearly shouted. "Like a person lying there dead!"

Tucker reeled back. His Adam's apple worked furiously. His body shook. "God, no! I didn't see anything! Nothing!"

Ray let the man sweat a bit longer. "Okay. You can go. We've got your number if we need to talk again."

Tucker didn't wait. He leaped up and rushed out.

Ray rubbed his chin. "So he heard something that could've been someone scaling the gate. This was about forty-five minutes before Drake left. That's a pretty high gate. If someone did come in that way, he would have to be pretty agile and strong. I'll get Atkins to check the area."

"We can do that ourselves."

"Yeah. Okay."

"You do realize we're going to have to interview each and every one of these people."

"How many are there?

Jimmy did a quick count. "About seventy-five."

"Gonna be a pain in the ass."

"Has to be done. Someone might've gone out for a smoke and seen or heard something." Jimmy imagined the tedious exercise ahead and made a decision. "We'll parcel out most of it. Bring in some of the night shift."

Ray grinned. "Sweet."

When they returned to the CVU, Novak was waiting for them. On a counter was a large black bag, digital camera, cell phone, tablet and a handbag that had held her personal effects.

"No wallet? Ray asked.

"No wallet," Novak responded.

"So he grabbed that and ran."

"Looks that way."

"We'll examine everything back at the station," Wyatt said.

"There was a silver SUV on Bayside that looked like it was sitting overnight. So we ran the plates. It's Drake's," Novak said.

Wyatt nodded. "Well, that confirms it then."

Jimmy went over the Bishop and Tucker interviews with him.

"You think we're just looking at a robbery gone sideways?"

"Probably," Ray said.

Jimmy said nothing.

Wyatt looked around. "We done here?"

"Yep."

"Then let's get rolling, boys."

"We'll be along in a bit," Ray said. "We're gonna check out the area around the gate."

Their search turned up nothing. The concrete had been washed clean by the overnight rain.

They missed the faint bicycle tracks in the soft dirt a few meters away.

Twenty-three

Back at the station, Robyn Lewitski was already fielding phone calls. Tongues had begun wagging with what little could be found on the radio and social media sites. It was her job to give out the standard information. "Yes, a body had been found. No, the victim has not been identified. Yes, we'll release a statement when we have more details. Until that time, we have no further comment."

The incident room had been set up, but at the moment all hands were in the kitchen wolfing down food that Adam Berry had retrieved from Justine's. Fortunately, the sandwich orders had been called in, relieving him of the necessity to wait and perhaps be assailed with questions from patrons. Anything out of the ordinary happening at the police station was food of a different sort.

Taking a half-eaten sandwich with him, Jimmy sat at a computer searching sites in vain for Diane Drake. The only record of her existence was the listing at the newspaper. "Her cellphone only has calls pertaining to work. Not one personal call." He was baffled. "She's almost invisible," he said to Ray, who sat at his desk working a bristled pick between his teeth. "You could write her bio on a postage stamp.

Usually you can find something on Facebook."

"Well, you won't find me on any of those sites," Ray said, removing the pick and inspecting it for stray bits. "And I'll bet you're not on there, either."

"You're right. I'm not."

"See? We're smart," Ray said. "But some people just can't keep away from that crap. Once you get on, you can't get off. And your privacy is gone forever. I'll take the old ways of the old days."

Jimmy had heard it all before and ignored him. "Contacting the editor of the paper seems to be the only way to get Drake's address and maybe her next of kin."

Ray looked at his watch. "He might be home. I wonder if he has his phone listed. If I was the editor of a local paper, I sure as hell wouldn't. Everyone would be calling to report this or that, or bitch about something. It would be like living in a fishbowl."

Jimmy got busy tapping his keyboard. "Nope. Nothing. Just an e-mail address at the paper."

"There was media at the site. He's probably aware of what's going on. Might even be there himself."

"I'll send him a message and ask him to come in for a chat."

It wasn't until after the service that Kittridge checked his e-mail to see if Nate had done any follow-up at the scene. Seeing a message from his favourite cop, he was caught off guard. *That's interesting. Nate must be right. Something big is going on at Heritage Gardens. I wonder why they want to talk to me?* Then he remembered that Diane had been on assignment there the previous evening. He suddenly felt very cold.

Edith came up to him standing in the foyer. "Hi. What did you think of the choir?"

Momentarily caught between his fears and his wife's question, he hesitated. "Sorry honey. Something strange has come up. I think you'll have to go to the Nineteenth Hole without me."

"Why? What's happened."

He explained Nate's earlier message and the request by the police. "It has to do with some kind of incident at Heritage Gardens. But what that's got to do with me I can't imagine," he added lightly.

"Then you'll be missing that fabulous brunch."

"Yeah. I was looking forward to it. My stomach already thinks my throat's cut. Maybe this thing at the station won't take long and I can still get there." But he knew in his heart that that was a lie.

Kittridge was now sitting in Chief Wyatt's office, digesting the news rather than lunch. Examining the photograph, he acknowledged that it was Diane Drake's face. His own face was drawn and pale.

"We need her address, Keith," Wyatt said. "You understand that we have to search her residence."

Kittridge reeled it off, Jimmy wrote it down, left the room, and returned as quickly as he left.

"And we need her next of kin."

Kittridge looked down, fingers of one hand working his mouth.

Ray and Jimmy glanced at each other, wondering why it was taking him so long to reply.

He looked up, anxiety on his face. "That's going to be a problem."

"Why's that?"

"Before I say too much more, I have to make a phone call."

Wyatt stared at Kittridge while considering his request. "Why's that?"

"It's a complicated situation. But what I *will* tell you is this. Diane Drake is not Diane Drake. Now, if you'll excuse me, I have to make that call." He walked out, leaving the officers with his jaw-dropping revelation.

Twenty-four

Some minutes later, Kittridge returned and sheepishly took his seat in front of Wyatt, directly in line with his withering gaze. It took some cajoling, but they finally got an outline of how Diane Drake came to Britannia Bay. But that was all. Kittridge was being chary with information and unwilling to reveal anything but the barest of details.

"So, let me get this straight," Wyatt started, using an old cop cliché that had Ray and Jimmy surreptitiously grinning at the floor. "You get a call from someone who tells you that he has a reporter to fill the slot left by Malcolm MacDonald."

"That's right. And it turned out that she was an arts columnist, which was even better."

Wyatt briefly went off message. "Bet you were happy to see the back of that git."

"Me *and* my lawyers." Kittridge's mouth was either a grin or a grimace. Wyatt couldn't decide. He returned to the matter at hand.

"But this man—I'm assuming it was a man—tells you that a person from Edmonton has to *bring* her here because he has to explain the issues that come with her employment."

"That's right."

"What sort of issues?"

"I didn't know the details. Only that she had to work under a *nom de plume*. But that isn't unusual in our business. What was unusual was that at any moment she might have to pack up and leave."

"So the person you called is on his way here?"

"Yes."

Before Wyatt could ask who the person was, or get an answer about Diane Drake's real name, the intercom light on his desk phone lit up. "Yes, Robyn?"

Ray and Jimmy watched as Wyatt's face began to flush. "Who?" he thundered. Hearing the confirmation, he scowled. There was only one person who elicited that response in Wyatt. Ray and Jimmy exchanged a knowing glance. "Send him in," Wyatt growled.

Corporal Ike Griffin was Wyatt's *bête noire*. For many years, the Britannia Bay Police Department had had to call on the RCMP for forensic help. And it always managed to be Griffin coming to the rescue. The last time they had crossed swords had been two years before during the murder investigation. Wyatt was reluctant to ask for assistance, as he despised being seen as the underdog. Furthermore, he suspected that Griffin was romantically involved with Dr. D., about whom he had proprietorial feelings.

At least now the department had a Mobile Crime Vehicle, solving one prickly situation. It was the other that caused Wyatt the most distress. Yes, he was devoted to his wife, Sherilee. But Dayani Nayagam was a thing apart—an exotic species that lured him in like an insect to a Venus flytrap. And the rumor that Griffin had cornered her affections aroused the green monster of jealousy in Wyatt.

He stared up at the man, younger than he was by a half dozen years or so, and trimmer and fitter, and, Wyatt grudgingly admitted to himself, handsome. Dark hair, dark eyes, square jaw—the whole nine yards. And if the occasion arose, which was highly unlikely around Wyatt, dimples that would set female hearts aflutter when he smiled. The only flaw was the slight pitting of teen-age acne on his face. To accent his youth, he was wearing a pair of chinos with a light tan windbreaker and topsider shoes.

"Chief Wyatt," he said softly—always softly—in his slight Texas accent, a remnant of his early life in that state.

"You know everyone here, Griffin. Take a seat and enlighten us. Who is Diane Drake and what brought her here?"

Before answering, he looked at Keith. "I'm sorry you had to be dragged into this, Keith. There was always the chance that she would be found, even in a remote place like Britannia Bay."

"What are you talking about? Found? Found by whom?" Wyatt demanded.

Griffin turned to Wyatt. "I'll give you some background."

Twenty-five

Edmonton, December 2015

The drummer gave a little "ka-thunk" on the bass drum, bringing the set to a close. After the applause sputtered and died, the audience got drinks and waited for the music to begin again after a twenty-minute break.

As Elaine prepared to leave, Ray Mah, owner of The Cellar, wove his way around tables to get to her. "You can't leave now, babe," he pleaded. "Things are just getting hot."

"That may be, but I have a day job, you know—unlike a lot of these folks," she tossed her head towards the patrons as she snatched up a woolen scarf and began to wrap it around her neck.

"So, what did you think of The Four Front?"

Elaine smirked. "You're wondering what I'm going to say in my column, aren't you? You know I never give anything away. You'll just have to buy a paper, or read it online."

"But they're great, aren't they? Especially Damian Graham. He plays the drums like they're musical instruments. His brush work is sublime."

She laughed. "With your way with words, maybe *you* should be writing the column."

He hesitated, contemplating his next words. "Well, *mine* wouldn't be so mean"

She gave him a quizzical look. "What do you mean, 'mean'?"

"Well, you know, you have to have empathy for musicians who are out there busting their butts for chump change."

"I'm assuming you have someone in mind."

"Yeah. I do. That young piano player who was just filling in a couple of weeks ago."

"Oh. Him. Well, the sweat *was* flying off him. I thought his fingers would slide off the keys."

Ray shook his head, then smiled. "You are *so* bad. Anyway, don't forget to mention where the guys come from. Lots of good jazz coming out of Vancouver Island."

"I know. I know." She interrupted and purposefully looked at her watch. While not wanting to stifle his enthusiasm, she knew that once on this train of thought he would start going on and on about performers.

"Okay. Okay. I get the not-so-subtle hint." He helped her on with her long, down-filled coat, then leaned in and grazed her cheek with a kiss. "See you soon?"

"You can count on it," she said, pulling up her fur-trimmed hood and tugging on her fleece-lined mittens.

"I heard that it's started to snow, so be careful." He opened the heavy door to a stairway leading up to yet another door at the street level.

The Cellar was an apt name for the jazz club located as it was in the basement of one of the refurbished old warehouses. This had once been a vibrant and bustling area of commerce, with trains dropping off boxcar after boxcar of merchandise and grain. But the railyards were phased out of operation in 1988 and by 1996 most of the freight sheds had been demolished.

Seeing its share of decay over the decades, the neighbourhood was slowly experiencing an influx of new money, since land for development was becoming scarce. Most of the remaining warehouses were restored and divided into offices, trendy restaurants and artists' lofts. The upscale change became a flashpoint for the homeless, who had found shelter within their walls and protested at being turfed out

Mah had had the foresight to get in on the ground floor—in this case it *was* the ground floor—and fulfill his dream of owning a jazz club. Although gentrification was gradually taking hold, this section of the warehouse district was still in transition and being avoided by all except the most dedicated jazz fans, or late-night drinkers and diners.

With each step up to the street level, the warmth from the club rapidly tapered off. Elaine pushed open the heavy door. A blast of bitter wind and icy snowflakes threatened to freeze her nostrils. She pulled the scarf across her nose and yanked the hood farther forward. Bundled up from head to toe, she felt cozy enough, but would have welcomed night-vision goggles to prevent the flakes from sticking to her eyelids. Conscious of the ice underfoot, she walked gingerly along the narrow one-way street.

About to cross the entrance to an alley between two buildings, Elaine heard loud male voices arguing in Arabic. She halted. The guttural sounds were becoming more and more familiar to the citizens of Alberta as Somali refuges arrived in the province, dreaming of well-paying jobs in Fort McMurray's oil-sands industry. Unfortunately, lacking the language and necessary skills, most young men ended up either driving cabs or doing other menial jobs. Or being unemployed altogether. Needing money to help support their parents and siblings, they were lured to the drug trade by other Somalis who told them stories about making $5,000 a day selling crack and cocaine. Then, when the deadly forest fire turned most of Fort McMurray into ash, they left for other cities. Their incursion into established illicit drug trade venues led to violent turf wars. The murder rate soared throughout the province.

While Elaine didn't understand the words, she recognized the anger behind them. Their intensity frightened her. Her car was on the other side of the alley. If she crossed the opening she might be seen. As she scrambled to think of what to do, a gunshot echoed off the walls. Someone would be running out, but which way? Toward the busy bars and restaurants at the other end of the alley? No. He'd be coming out a few feet from her.

It was too late to run back to The Cellar. She had one option. Pressing herself against the building she waited, terrified, face against the concrete, heart hammering against her breastbone. Seconds later, footsteps of at least two people ran by. Car doors opened and closed. An engine turned over, wheels spun, then gripped and sped off.

Praying that everyone had cleared out and the danger had passed, she ran into the alley, certain that someone would be wounded. Or worse. She saw a man lying on his back, moaning, a pool of blood already beginning to congeal from the cold. She crouched beside him. His breathing was shallow. She pulled the scarf away from her mouth. "I'm getting help." As she fumbled with her cumbersome mittens trying to reach for her cellphone, she realized that would be a stupid move. Then she heard him struggling to say something. She bent closer.

"Ja-bril," he whispered.

"Do you have a cellphone?"

He made no response. His breath was now rattling. Coagulating blood covered a ragged tear in his coat. *He must have a cellphone.* His left pocket was visible. She removed her right mitten. Fingers stinging from the cold, she reached in, but there was nothing. She moved around his body and found a cellphone in his other pocket. She entered 9-1-1, then tugged on her mitten and yanked up her scarf.

"This is the 9-1-1 operator. What is your emergency?"

"A man's been shot," she said with her mouth muffled. She quickly gave the location. As the operator was asking for her information, Elaine ended the call and placed the phone by the victim's side. It seemed an eternity before she heard the *wa-wa* of the ambulance in the distance, but it was no more than five minutes. "Help is coming," she told him, then bolted out of the alley and into her car, racing for home.

Twenty-six

After a night spent more awake than asleep, Elaine rolled out of bed just before six o'clock. She clicked on the morning talk show and lowered the yakking sounds of the hosts until the camera switched to the news reader.

"We have breaking news. A shooting took place in the warehouse district last night. It's believed to be connected to the illegal drug trade. A man with a gunshot wound was taken to hospital where he later died of his injuries. Chief of Police Jake Chalmers will be holding a press briefing later this morning to give further details."

Listening to the report, she felt a slight pang of sorrow, then fear, as she realized that the police would surely be looking for the witness who called 9-1-1. Would they say anything at the briefing? She made coffee, had breakfast, and sat in thought. After she had showered and dressed, she called her boss at *The Edmonton Times*.

"Good morning, Henry. I just heard the news of the homicide last night. There's going to be a police briefing. I was wondering if I could cover that."

There was a long pause. "That's way off your beat, Elaine. What's your interest?"

She had her story ready. "Well, I was at The Cellar last night. This morning I got an e-mail from Ray Mah telling me a murder took place not far from the club around the time I left. I'm thinking of weaving it into my review."

A raucous guffaw pierced her ear. "Damn, Elaine! That's a bit macabre, don't you think?"

"Maybe. But do you already have someone assigned to it?"

"Not yet." Another pause. "If you want to cover it, go ahead. Do you know the Media Liaison?"

"No."

"Well, just keep your head down and your ears open. And don't ask any dumb questions. In fact, don't ask any questions at all. They're not going to reveal more than what's in the release. So get a copy of that."

"Okay. When is it?"

She heard a rustle of paper and imagined the mess on Henry's desk. How he could put out a paper every day, with all the correct facts and figures, was an ongoing topic of conversation among the staff over pints at The Craft Beer Market. "It's at 11:30."

The snowfall had ended. The December sky was clear. The air was cold and windy. Temperature, minus twenty. Celsius. Who knew what it was with the wind chill? Bundled up once again, Elaine left her car plugged into a block heater and jumped on the handy LRT, making it to the police station in good time. Not having attended a briefing before, she approached a uniformed woman at reception, showed her press credentials and asked for the briefing's location.

With all the warmth of a polar ice cap, the woman replied, "Room 110. You'll be scanned. No electronic devices allowed." She pointed to the right. "Down the hall."

Elaine thanked her and smiled. Reporters were treated like

pariahs by the police everywhere. A little bit of courtesy was no skin off her teeth and might even soften the woman's attitude toward the press. Somehow, she doubted it.

Following instructions, she handed over her cellphone, removed her coat and turned out her pockets. While she was being scanned, her bag was searched by another officer. Thank God it was a woman, she thought, picturing all the female paraphernalia in her stash of stuff. The officer handed her a lanyard with "Press" on it. Elaine hung it around her neck. Getting the okay, she put her coat back on, since the police station was as frosty as their receptionist. Entering Room 110, she was handed an official Press Release. She quickly made her way to a row of chairs near the back. Among the television crews were a few journalists she knew. One looked at her with questioning eyes. Most likely he knew this was not her traditional beat.

Before Elaine had time to read the handout, Chief Chalmers entered through a side door, followed by the female Media Liaison, who took the dais. After a preamble, she handed the mike to Chalmers. While he gave an outline of the facts, Elaine's mind wandered to the previous evening. It wasn't until he mentioned the word "witness," that her ears perked up.

"The 9-1-1 operator received an anonymous tip concerning the presence of a wounded man, but ended the call before giving a name or contact number. We would like this person to come forward and assure him or her of the full confidentiality of their information. For obvious reasons, it will not be made known to the public. But the victim may have said something to the witness. He was known to the police and associated with individuals in the drug trade." Chalmers gave a number the witness could call and mentioned that it was on the Press Release.

Elaine's hands had turned cold and she felt her heart beating through her layers of clothing. She wanted to leave, but knew she needed to wait until all the reporters had a chance to ask their questions. As Henry had implied, many were just plain stupid.

After his patience had expired, Chalmers transferred the mike back to his spokesperson and left the room. After a quick wrap-up, everyone cleared out.

Her legs a bit unsteady, Elaine took a few moments to gather herself together and made her way down the hall and out the door. Arriving at the paper, she handed the Press Release to Henry, who noticed her shaking hand. He looked up at her. "Are you all right, Elaine? You look like you've seen a ghost."

"I'm not feeling well, Henry."

"Then for God's sake, go home. Don't worry about the briefing. We'll cobble something together."

She went into the women's washroom, entered a cubicle and waited while someone finished washing her hands, and then left. She took out her cellphone and, rather than calling the number given out by Chief Chalmers, she called one of her own contacts. He answered right away.

"Hi, my friend. How are you this cold and blowy day?"

"Dave, we have to meet."

Hearing the urgency in her voice, he didn't hesitate. "Right. Same time? Same place?"

She was sitting in the back booth of a diner, nursing a lukewarm coffee. The place had seen better days, but it was still serving up good comfort food and equally good coffee. No one came here for trendy cuisine. When the waitress asked if she would like a top up, Elaine shook her head. "Maybe later, Rose. I'm waiting for Dave," she told her.

"We're still serving dinner, Elaine. Would you like a menu?" She said "dinner," not "lunch," causing Elaine to smile. Her mother, daughter of prairie farmers, always called the noonday meal "dinner."

And the evening meal was "supper." There was no such mealtime word as "lunch" in their lexicon. "Lunch" was what you took in your pail to work or school.

She nodded. "Okay." Rose, not a day under sixty-five and still working, returned with two menus just as Dave Young came through the door.

Removing his heavy leather jacket, he smiled at the waitress. "Hi, Rose." She gestured with the coffee pot. "Yeah, I'll have a cup, thanks."

"How about you, honey? Are you ready for that top up?"

"I'm afraid I've let it get cold."

"No problem." She dropped the menus on the table, took Elaine's cold coffee and returned with a hot one. "Take your time ordering what you want. The specials are the same today as they were yesterday, and the day before that, and probably into the next century," she snickered.

"I'll have the mac and cheese and cole slaw."

"Extra cheddar?"

"Extra cheddar."

She picked up the menus and turned to Elaine. "You're not going to force him to eat alone, are you?"

"I'll have what he's having."

When he and Rose laughed it took a couple of seconds for Elaine to twig to the restaurant scene from *When Harry met Sally*. She managed a grin.

With Rose off taking care of their order, Young gave Elaine a good, hard look. "What's up, girl?" He took one of her hands.

Leaning across the table, she whispered, "That murder last night. *I* called it in. *I* was the witness." She knew he would know about it. Dave worked for CSIS: the Canadian Security and Intelligence Service. "And he said something before the ambulance got there. He said 'Jabril'. The police need that information, but obviously *I* can't give it to them. And I don't know if was his name or the killer's."

Young released her hand and rested his head on the vinyl-covered padding. Elaine could almost see his brain spinning. After a minute or two he told her that he would get that information to the police. But before he could say anything further, Rose arrived with the food. He switched gears, making a great show of breathing in the steam rising from the mac and cheese. "Smells heavenly, Rose."

"Just like your mother used to make, right?"

"This ain't no Kraft dinner."

"You got that right," she chuckled and walked away.

He tucked in right away, seemingly famished. Elaine watched, fascinated as usual with the way he ate. He could win an eating contest if it was based on speed. And yet, he didn't seem to be gobbling his food. He ate with precision. Looking down at her plate, she didn't think she could eat at all. But the first forkful dispelled that thought. The mac and cheese was rich and creamy and seemed to soothe her nerves.

After wiping his mouth with a napkin, Young pushed aside his empty plate. "I can tell you right now that Jabril was not the name of the victim. He was fingering Jabril Barre. Barre's a Somali immigrant who's now one of the biggest and most ruthless drug dealers in Alberta. He's one of the kids of the generation that fled Somalia two decades ago. They're called *ciyaal baraf.* Children of the snow. He started off in Fort McMurray, where about 3,000 of them lived at one time. But with the town basically burned down, he's parked his sorry ass here. He's been busted a couple of times, but unfortunately he's got a top-notch lawyer who always manages to get him off.

Elaine shivered. "And there's a gang war going on now, isn't there?"

Dave nodded.

"And Jabril's going to be wondering who this witness is. And at that time of night, who would be around? People leaving bars. People leaving The Cellar. If he's as dangerous as you say, won't he lean on Ray or the owners of the other places that were open at that time of night?"

"It's a possibility, but on the other hand, he would be tipping his hand by alerting everybody. He might just lay low."

His words proved to be wrong. She was at her desk the following week, when she heard a colleague saying, "Ray Mah."

Her head shot up. "What's that about Ray?"

"Oh, right. That's your bailiwick, isn't it, Elaine?"

She went over to him. "What's happened?" Her throat was tight with fear.

"He was beat up last night after the club closed. Some thugs worked him over and trashed the place."

"Oh, my God!" She had purposely not written the review of The Four Front so as not to give away the fact that she had been there the night of the murder. She had been protecting herself. But why hadn't Dave seen to it that Ray had police protection? She grabbed her cellphone, called him from the hallway, but was directed to his voicemail. Gritting her teeth, she left a message saying that Ray had been attacked and she was going to the hospital. Back in the office she slipped into her coat, preparing to leave. Her cellphone buzzed.

"Don't go near the hospital, Elaine," Dave said. "They'll have people watching to see who visits him."

"But that's awful, Dave. I'm responsible in a way. And I'm sure Ray has put two and two together and figured out it was me." She felt a chill pass through her body. "Jesus, what if he told them it was *me* who left around the time of the murder? What if they beat it out of him? They'll come for me next." She was shaking.

"Go home. No. Better yet, I'll pick you up in fifteen minutes."

Twenty-seven

They had been talking—arguing was more like it—for over an hour. Now they sat staring at each other across Dave's kitchen table, heels dug in on both sides. One or the other was going to have to concede. Elaine blinked. "But where will I go?"

"I'll find a safe place for you. I've got contacts from one end of the country to the other."

"But what about work? I have to work. And no one is hiring reporters these days with all the papers closing or consolidating."

Dave looked off, thinking. After several minutes, he turned back to her with conviction on his face. "I'll find someone who can solve both problems."

"But what can I tell Henry?"

"I'll talk to him; tell him the truth."

"But what about Mom? Will *she* be safe?"

"Yes. Different name. Different city. She'll be all right."

She thought about her mother changing her name as soon as her husband had been declared legally dead. Elaine often wished she had done the same thing, but her name was well known now, and to change it would only have caused confusion.

"But what do I do with my condo?"

"Do you have the right to sublet?"

"Yes."

"Okay. Let us handle that. We can easily find someone to take over the lease."

"But for how long, Dave?" She felt that she was running out of arguments.

"As long as it takes. Barre will get protection from his gang or his family, or any of their knowns across Canada. We could be looking at several months. Maybe a year."

"A year?!"

Dave reached for her hands as her shock turned to despair. "It may not to be that long, Elaine. He'll be found eventually. Someone may give him up, especially if there's a financial incentive to do so."

She looked at him, sorrow and worry etched on her face. With the last of her challenges neutralized, she crossed the Rubicon.

Twenty-eight

Back in Britannia Bay

That's quite a story, Corporal Griffin," Wyatt began. "You would have us believe that Diane . . . uh . . . Elaine Monford was in some kind of witness protection program and you think the thugs tracked her down and killed her?"

"I don't know if that's the case, but she *was* in the program. It was what brought her here. She lived in fear of being discovered."

Kittridge jumped in. "He's right. She was wrapped tighter than a Tootsie Roll."

"So how did you become involved, Griffin?"

"I was contacted by an old friend who works for CSIS—"

"CSIS!" Wyatt cut him off.

Ray exchanged a glance with Jimmy. This was becoming curiouser and curiouser.

Griffin ignored his outburst. "He said he was looking for a safe place for Monford. Some place where she could work as a journalist. It was no secret that Keith wanted to get rid of MacDonald."

"I thought she was the answer to my prayers, frankly," Kittridge mumbled.

"So who is this friend of yours?"

"His name is Dave Young. I knew him from the time he was in the RCMP. We've kept in touch."

Ray and Jimmy had been listening to the narrative. Ray cleared his throat. "Chief," he interjected.

Wyatt looked at him, expecting him to say something. But what he got was Ray gesturing with an upturned hand and raised eyebrows.

Wyatt nodded. Then he turned to Griffin. "I'm sorry to inform you, but it's our opinion, based on the facts, that Elaine Monford was not murdered by some professional hit men. There's no way this was a contract killing. It has all the appearance of a botched robbery. If it had been a hit, there'd have been a weapon used—a gun or a knife. Something. But she had a broken jaw and the back of her head was bashed in from landing on the pavement. So, whoever it was just knocked her off her feet, dragged her into the bush and stole her wallet. That's what we've got."

Griffin took in this information. Then he shook his head. "I can't believe it was random. But I'll leave it to you to solve." He got up to go.

"Hang on a minute, Griffin. I need a next of kin."

"I can't help you there, but Young will know. He'll be here tomorrow morning."

"Well, I look forward to his arrival," Wyatt said, dryly.

"Would you let me know when I can put something in the paper?" Kittridge had the temerity to ask.

Wyatt stopped himself from uttering an epithet. "You'll have to cool your heels for a while, Kittridge."

"I figured that."

"And fax over whatever relevant information you have on Drake to Dr. Dayani."

After they left, a whoosh of air escaped Wyatt's lungs. "This is some mystery. It looked like a robbery, plain, but maybe not so simple.

Now with this added information . . ." He shrugged. "Maybe this CSIS guy can shed some light on it," he said, massaging the back of his neck.

Jimmy spoke up. "Ariel told me that Diane Drake was hated by the arts community. Apparently, some of her reviews were pretty vitriolic."

Ray guffawed. "C'mon Jimmy. You don't think some limp-wristed violinist could break a jaw, do you?"

Jimmy thought about how heavy some of the instruments were, but made no further comment.

Wyatt pushed himself out of his chair. "I'm going to wait to hear from this Young character. First the bloody RCMP and now spies. What the hell is going on here? We need to know a lot more about this Monford woman, that's for sure. Maybe the SOCOs will find something at her apartment."

In Edmonton, when the field supervisor learned that Elaine Monford's required morning check-in call had not been received, she called Dave Young, whose team moved into action. Within the hour, they had gained access to Monford's apartment, swept it, removed the bugging devices and left with her laptop and CSIS-encrypted cellphone.

Twenty-nine

Wyatt drove a different way to his home in the Township. It was his custom to take the shorter of the two routes because he was always anxious to get home to his wife, and his den. With her, and in there, he found solace from his stressful job. Today, however, he meandered along the bay thinking, and drinking in the spring sunshine, and watching people with their dogs splashing in and out of the water. It was a glorious Easter Sunday, one he wished he could enjoy.

This murder was as murky as the shadows lurking in the back of his mind. Moreover, outside forces were encroaching on his territory, one he took pains to protect. He was afraid they would break through its boundaries, spreading the investigation far afield and out of his control. How could he prevent that from happening? What would be unearthed from Dave Young, CSIS whatever. Undercover agent? What was his role in this? And who the hell was Elaine Monford when she was home?

Ray sat at the kitchen table, belching quietly now and then after a late lunch of antipasto and lasagne. He was presently dunking one of his daughter's biscotti into his espresso and thinking that it was very good. Just as good as Lana's. Georgina walked in, dressed for work. Sunday was always a busy day at Catalani's and Easter Sunday saw more than its regular patrons due to its *prezzo fisso* meal featuring roast leg of lamb with garlic and rosemary.

Ray held up the biscotti. "She's nailed these."

Georgina smiled. "Yes, she has."

"Too bad the restaurant doesn't have a bigger kitchen for her to work in."

"About that," she began, and sat beside him. "The florist next door is planning to sell out. She can't compete with Bayside Foods anymore." She made a silent prayer, then continued. "We're thinking we should buy her place, then knock out the walls and renovate."

"What?!" Ray dropped the rest of the biscotti into his cup. "That would mean closing for a couple of months, at least. And where's the money supposed to come from?"

"Calm down, big boy. We've already had a discussion about it and figured out we could manage it."

"'We'? What 'we'? Where am I in this 'we'?"

She ignored his umbrage. "Ray, you're busy being a cop. And besides, you're not involved in the day-to-day running of the restaurant. You haven't a clue about what goes on past the dining area. You eat there. That's it. The books look good. Papa and I are going to talk to Bob at the bank next week. I'm sure we can swing it."

"This is moving along pretty fast, Georgina."

"It only seems that way for you, Ray. We've spent the last month tossing it around."

"Why didn't you include me?" he asked, smarting from feelings of exclusion.

"Because Catalani's is not your concern," she said, as kindly as possible.

But Ray was in a mood. "If it concerns the family, it concerns *me*."

She waited out his petulance. "If we can manage it, what's your problem?"

He grabbed a spoon and fished the biscotti from his cup, and turned from chewing on that to chewing on his lips as he thought about what she was telling him. Georgina was patient, knowing he would acquiesce. He just needed a moment to look at the overall picture. "When do you plan to close? Not in the summer, I hope. That's when we rake in the most money."

"Well, if we get the financing, we can start right away. It will most likely cross over into June, but July and August are our busiest months. Hopefully it would be ready by then."

"Okay. But what are you going to do when the place is closed?"

"Well . . ." Her face took on a coquettish look, sending off Ray's warning signals. "I thought *we* could go to Pesaro for a month or so. You, me and Gabby. Visit Leonora and Serena."

Ray's mind instantly pictured Serena, the toddler who landed on their laps when Leonora decided she needed to "sort out" her life, and left her baby behind. A year later, when she returned to claim her daughter, Ray and Georgina had been broken-hearted and angry. They loved Serena as though she were their own flesh and blood. There had been shouting matches and threats. Silvana and Umberto had had to step in to throw oil on the waters in order to prevent a split in the family. They were afraid it might make Serena inaccessible to them in the future. That was twenty-one years ago, and with time, the rancour was forgotten, especially after Marcus and Gabriella arrived to fill the void.

"You know, a trip to Pesaro would be really nice," he agreed. "But first, I've got a crime to solve. So maybe you go and I'll join you when it's wrapped up. I think it's already a slam dunk."

"Sounds like a plan," she smiled.

"What plan?" Marcus asked, sauntering in.

"We're going to Italy. Me, your mom and Gabby," Ray replied, looking at his handsome nineteen-year-old son. Georgina had told Ray how Marcus had turned a lot of heads in church that morning, and it was easy to see why. When he had been featured on the front page of *The Bayside Bugle* during the grad parade two years before, girls began depleting their data usage, calling him. Ray pictured a lot of broken hearts in the future.

"Italy, huh. Cool. When are you going?"

"At the end of next month, if all goes smoothly." She explained the restaurant renovations and the expectations of spending time with Leonora and Serena.

"What about The Ravens?" Marcus asked.

Ray could have kicked himself. So caught up with thoughts of Italy, he hadn't even considered his peewee baseball team. He made a face. "I suppose I'll have to let Jack step up to the plate," he said, picturing Jack Johnson, his skinny assistant, who was more apt to coddle than coach. "We should be back before he's done too much damage."

"You hope." Marcus laughed, then stopped. "Have you told Gabby yet?"

"Not yet. Why?"

"I don't think she'll want to leave her boyfriend."

"Her boyfriend!" Ray thundered.

"Yeah. Russ Martin."

"I thought I put an end to that."

"Dad." Marcus drew out the word and shook his head. "Anytime you tell people who think they're in love that they can't see each other, it only drives them closer together. You should know that. It's Psych 101."

"And *Romeo and Juliet*," Georgina added.

"In love?" Ray said, sarcastically. "What does she know about that?"

"You're sounding like a Neanderthal, Ray."

"Well, what am I going to do about it? He doesn't seem like the kind of guy she deserves."

"You don't even know him, Dad. He's not your bookish type, but he's smart with his hands. He fixes all the cars for my friends and doesn't charge them anything except for parts. He's a good guy. Give him some slack."

"Well, she's coming with us to Italy whether she likes it or not. If they're so *in love*, they can be apart for a few weeks. And besides, she'll be able to text him and send him e-mails. So, it won't be a hardship for her to spend time with her aunt and cousin. And who knows what exposing her to Italian culture will do?" And he hoped to some nice Italian boys as well.

Molly hurtled herself from the floor to the counter to the top of the refrigerator and made herself comfortable as she watched her mistress sweeping a liquid on top of meat with a tiny broom. She lifted a paw, licked it and began swiping it across her ears. Ariel put down the basting brush and reached up to grab her, but Molly was too quick, leaping to the floor and dashing down the hallway to the bedroom.

"Honestly, that cat," Ariel said to Jimmy, who had lowered the crossword puzzle to watch the scene.

He smiled. "She's part Siamese, part monkey. What do you expect?"

Roger dozed in his corner bed, oblivious to the racket around him.

"Will you set the table, honey? I'm going to change. And put out a wine glass for Lilah, too."

"She doesn't drink wine."

"I know, but it'll be nice to have her apple juice in a wine glass, don't you think?"

He gave her a warm smile. "You're sweet. You know that?"

"Yes. I know that."

"Cheeky."

Lana had been planning on eating alone on Easter Sunday. She was often by herself, and didn't mind. But holidays that involved family and food left her wondering if her mother had been right. Perhaps she should have married and had children. But it was a thought that took immediate flight as she pictured the ramifications—the tyranny of small children; the sullenness of teenagers; the demands of daily life draining all your energy. She grimaced. That sort of life was not for her. Still, there was that lack of communal interaction. When Ariel had invited her for dinner, her heart gave a joyful leap. She packed up one of her "Legendary Lemon Pies," grabbed a bottle of Armagnac and headed out the door, humming.

After her husband, Melvin, died, it had been Delilah's habit to partake of the traditional Easter Sunday dinner at her church. But she had already been to church that day, and Ariel's cooking was infinitely more tempting. Jimmy once said that Ariel could give Lourdes a run for their money when it came to miracle cures for whatever ailed you. Delilah believed that. After she broke her wrist during the murder investigation two years before, it had been Ariel's meals that had nourished her before she decided to use Dinner At Your Doorstep. And hadn't that come to a strange end? She gave Tabitha a kiss on her head, wrestled her walker out the door, and made her way across the street.

"This is my version of Easter dinner, everyone," Ariel said, placing sliced ham in an apricot glaze, scalloped potatoes and grilled asparagus on the table. Delilah's dinner had been diced and put in a shallow bowl. Along with a spoon, it was her preferred way of eating, as her poor eyesight made it difficult to use a fork and knife. Often she would bring the fork up to her mouth only to find there was nothing on it.

"Thank you, Ariel," she said gratefully. And when Jimmy poured apple juice into her wine glass, she beamed. "At least this makes me feel like a grown up."

After he half-filled the other glasses with Gewürztraminer, he sat down and picked up his napkin.

"Do you mind if I say grace?" Delilah asked.

Knowing her devotion to her faith, they stopped what they were doing and bowed their heads.

Delilah intoned: "Grace's face is full of grace and Grace's nose is long. 'Twould be no disgrace to Grace's face if half her nose was gone."

Everyone burst out laughing.

"My mother taught me that one. She loved a poke at the Lord now and then. She thought He deserved a laugh after all His hard work."

The entrée had been polished off, the last of the wine drunk, and Lana's lemon pie had left them smacking their lips. Coffee and brandy followed, except for Jimmy, who rarely drank coffee after five o'clock, and distilled spirits never. Ariel and Lana had long ago stopped teasing him about his abstemious habits. Even Delilah enjoyed the apricot brandy that Ariel kept on hand for her.

As they relaxed, enjoying the contentment and camaraderie, Delilah couldn't hold back her curiosity any longer. "Are we allowed to ask any questions about the goings on at Heritage Gardens today?"

"You can ask me anything you want," he smiled at her.

"Asking is one thing. Answering is another. The only thing we know so far is that a body was taken away in an ambulance," she said.

"Nothing unusual about that."

"Well, my first question would be, was it a murder?"

"Gosh. Why would *that* be your first question, Lilah?" Ariel asked.

"Well, you know me. I like a bit of excitement to spice up my life."

At the word "murder" Lana's thoughts turned to the day she drove Delilah to the hospital and got herself entangled in the death of their neighbour. She gave an involuntary shiver.

Ariel noticed. "Maybe we shouldn't talk about this right now. It's not exactly the sort of conversation to have on Easter Sunday."

Lana interjected. "If you're stopping on my account, don't. I'm as curious as the next person." She carried on gamely. "So, what can you tell us?"

Knowing them well, Jimmy thought they could be relied on to keep mum. Still, he hesitated. "This is a puzzling investigation, so far. At least to me it is. But as usual, I'll have to remind you not to mention a word of it outside this house."

"You have my word," Delilah said.

"Mine, too."

"What about the cats?" Delilah asked.

"Well, I can vouch for Roger, " Jimmy said, "but I'm not so sure about Molly."

"Hey!" Ariel pounced. They all laughed.

"Okay, here's what we have so far." Jimmy began sketching a rough draft of facts and conjecture, beginning with the murder in Edmonton. At the end, they were as puzzled as he was. Finally, Delilah spoke.

"Well, here's my two-bits worth," she said. "I think the stolen wallet is a ruse to make the cops think it was a heist that went south." They chuckled at her choice of words, no doubt borrowed from one of her beloved police dramas.

Jimmy nodded. "That's my take on it. I think it was planned, but it wasn't a contract killing."

Delilah nodded. "Yeah. A hitman would've just whacked her."

That, and the brandy, got the women giggling again,

"So, give me some ideas," Jimmy said. "Diane Drake was in some kind of witness protection program because of what she saw in Edmonton. So, assuming it wasn't a professional hit, then who else wanted her dead?"

"If she was in a witness protection program, then that wasn't her real name, was it?" Lana said.

"No. It wasn't."

"What was it?"

"I can't tell you that."

"What did she do in Edmonton?" Delilah asked.

"Ah," said Jimmy. "This is the interesting point. She was an arts reporter."

"Well, as I told you after Irina's funeral," Ariel pointed out, "Diane Drake was hated for the way she savaged performers. Maybe this time the sword was mightier than the pen."

"But there was no weapon," Lana said.

"No."

"The perp's hands were the weapon," Delilah stated.

"You'd have to be strong to land a punch so hard it would kill someone." Ariel said.

"Not if you hit a person in the right place. And in this case, it was a combination of the punch and her head hitting the road," Jimmy said.

"Whatever. The person had to be strong," Lana agreed.

"So, you think it was a man that carried it out?"

"Of course," Ariel said with conviction.

The other two women nodded in agreement, certain that at least that much was settled.

Thirty

April 17th

Wyatt awoke to a gloomy, drizzly day, which matched his mood. He sat on the edge of the bed, contemplating the day, the year, his life.

Sherilee was about to walk in, but stopped at the doorway when she saw her husband's hunched back and drooped head. To her, it appeared to be a physical manifestation of what was eating at him. He had moped around the previous evening, offering grunts or one-word answers as his contribution to the conversation. It had even seemed an effort to comment on her Easter Sunday dinner. Normally he would have been effusive with praise.

"Bill?"

He turned to look at her, his face blank.

She went over and put her arms around him. "What's going on in that noggin of yours?"

He shook his head and sighed. "I've hit a wall, Sherilee."

"You mean this case?"

He stood and faced her. "That's only part of it. I've finally reached the point where I hate my job. I'm wondering if now's the time to pack it in."

"You've said that before, honey. And are you really ready for retirement? You still have a lot of years left."

"I don't know." He glanced away, then, after a moment, turned back to her. Sherilee was his high school sweetheart, and still was, in his eyes. Her hair might be grey and she had a few extra pounds around her middle, but so did he. They were growing old together and accepting the changes. For years the two of them had spread out maps on the dining table, planning their life after "freedom day," as they called it. They were going to sell the house, buy a motorhome and travel all over North America. It had been their dream. "But I *do* know that I want to crack this case. It's not making any sense. And I'm afraid it's going to be taken over by the RCMP. Or CSIS."

"CSIS?! What have *they* got to do with it?"

He shook his head. "I don't know that, either. But I'm going to find out more today. A CSIS guy from Edmonton is coming here to give me some background on Diane Drake, which I found out is not her real name. It's Elaine Monford. Of course, Keith Kittridge is involved." He paused. "But so is that damned Ike Griffin."

When she heard the name, she began to understand his state of mind. "Why don't you have a hot shower and get dressed? I'll make you poached eggs on toast and throw in some rashers of low-salt bacon. By then you should feel better."

He gave her a long hug. "What did I ever do to deserve you?"

"You were the only guy who didn't look at my boobs before looking at my face."

"Yeah," he laughed. "And that took a will of iron, I can tell you."

When Wyatt arrived at the station, some of his piss and vinegar had returned. It helped that the weather had improved and Mary Beth had picked up some Danishes from Justine's to go with his final cup of coffee of the day. He had learned his lesson two years before when his full bladder almost threw a wrench into an arrest. Draining the cup, he began reading over the case notes when she peeked around his half-opened door.

"Chief, there's a Dave Young in the lobby. He says he has an appointment with you."

"He's here already?" He jumped up and struggled to fasten the buttons of his uniform.

A tall, partly bald man of medium build stood in the foyer. He wore a tailored black blazer, white shirt open at the collar, dark gray slacks and shoes with a shine as glossy as satin. His skin was pale, but not pallid, and his alert eyes were a very light blue under eyebrows that sloped downward. A long nose and unremarkable jaw completed his face. Wyatt thought his nondescript features were perfect if he were a spy.

"Dave Young?"

"How do you do, Chief Wyatt. I apologize for arriving so early, but I was able to requisition a flight direct to your airport." His voice exuded confidence and fell easily on the ears. An energetic handshake topped off the first impressions.

Wyatt instinctively liked the man. He would be a disarming spy, he thought. "Really? Then you must be high on the chain of command," he laughed. "How did you get to the station?"

"Rental car."

"Would you like a coffee and Danish? We have a fresh brew system, so you don't have to worry about a bad cup."

"Sounds good. I didn't have time for breakfast this morning and the flight was a bit rough. Didn't want to chance spilling coffee on my pants."

Wyatt chuckled as he played host, dropping a coffee pod into the machine. Young took in the well-appointed kitchen that was larger than those found in most cop shops. "This is a pleasant surprise," he said, gesturing around the room.

"I fought hard for this," Wyatt said, as he put out the box of pastry, one small plate and utensils. "I like my men and women to feel at home here. We often take our meetings in this room. Do you take cream or milk?"

"No. Just black."

Wyatt placed the coffee on the table, then pointed to a chair. "Have a seat." He sat opposite Young

"You're not joining me?"

Wyatt shrugged. "Too much coffee. And I've already had a Danish. You know what it's like."

Young *did* know. It was difficult being a police chief, sitting at a desk most of the day, drinking endless cups of coffee, and eating the fabled doughnuts or other unhealthy food on the fly. He had also taken note of the straining buttons on Wyatt's jacket and wondered if, when, and how the chief exercised.

As they sat and made small talk, officers began filing in, shooting curious glances at the visitor. Wyatt had always made it a habit to keep his crew in the loop, and he would do so after Young had left. He made an exception for one troublesome constable who had a big mouth. When Ray and Jimmy walked in, he called them right over.

"Young, I'd like you to meet the two investigating officers on this case—Detective Sergeant Ray Rossini and D.S. Jimmy Tan." After the customary introductions, all four retired to Wyatt's office.

In the squad room, constables conferred.

"That must be the CSIS guy," Novak said.

"Have you noticed that he resembles a young Alec Guinness?" Rhys-Jones asked.

"I thought he looked like an older Nicholas Cage," Foxcroft said.

That was the discussion outside Wyatt's office. Inside, it was another story altogether.

Thirty-one

Wyatt reiterated Griffin's briefing about Monford's predicament in Edmonton while Young listened without commenting, only giving the occasional nod. When Wyatt finished, he finally spoke. "You have a good grasp of the events. There's really nothing I can add to that."

"So, with Monford still here, I'm assuming the RCMP never nabbed Barre."

"Not yet. But he's as good as gone. He might even have managed to slip out of the country on a false passport. We were beginning preparations for Elaine's return." He paused. "Unfortunately, we hadn't told her that."

There was a moment of quiet thought as the ramifications of that lapse sank in.

Wyatt cleared his throat. "What about notifying the next of kin? They'll have to identify the body. Have you contacted them yet?"

"Well, Chief Wyatt, the next of kin"—he said, making air quotations around the three words—"would have to be me, although Elaine and I were not related. Her mother lives in a care home now and is unable to travel. I am Power of Attorney for both her and Elaine and the Executor of Elaine's estate. I'll view her body and arrange for the transfer back to her hometown."

"She has no siblings or other family who could do this?"

"There were some relatives, but from what she told me they never kept in touch. It was clear her family was dysfunctional. Not only that, her father abused her and her mother. He disappeared when she was a teenager."

"Disappeared?" Ray's ears pricked up.

"That was what Mrs. Monford said. He was there one day and gone the next. But we had our suspicions."

Ray pressed. "But there *was* an investigation?"

"Yes. We weren't called in right away. I was working for the RCMP then. That's how I met Elaine."

Ray nodded. "I don't imagine it was all that thorough given the fact that he was abusive." He let that hang in the air.

Young fixed Ray with a look. "No. It wasn't. In fact, we didn't give a damn about the guy. He was known to be violent and we thought it was the best thing for Elaine and her mother that he didn't seem to be around any longer."

Ray smirked. "Of course, there was always the possibility that he would eventually show up."

A shade of a smile was Young's response.

The room went quiet. They were all familiar with the scenario. It was common in small, rural communities everywhere—people mysteriously missing, murders committed and not diligently investigated, particularly when the victim didn't merit much sympathy. "Good riddance to bad rubbish" often came before "Innocent until proven guilty."

It was Jimmy who spoke first. "If this is not a robbery gone wrong, and not a professional hit, can you think of any reason why Miss Monford was targeted?"

It took a while before Young answered. "She had had a couple of threats from disgruntled readers in Edmonton, but that goes with the territory. Not everyone is happy with a review. Although I will say, some were pretty nasty."

"That what we've heard here, too," Wyatt said. "I mean, not that there were threats, but there were complaints. She seemed to have a real stick up her ass when it came to classical music."

"Well, there's a valid reason for that," Young said. "And it was the one thing that made me suspicious about her father's so-called disappearance. The neighbours told us that the loud music suddenly stopped. Seems he was a fan of classical music and he would turn it up full tilt. This was an area that preferred country and western, so you can imagine that he was none too popular with the folks who lived around there." He paused. "When we scoured the property, we found bits of old LPs near the garbage cans. And there wasn't one record inside the house."

They absorbed the information.

"When you searched Elaine's apartment, did you find anything useful?" Young asked them. He already knew the answer to that, but had to feign ignorance.

"No. According to the SOCOs, her place was like a motel. She didn't even have a computer. Just a TV. She had an iPad and cellphone in her bag."

Young nodded. "Let me know when her personal belongings are ready to be packed up. I'll have someone do that and also take care of the shipping."

"Okay. We'll be holding on to her iPad and cellphone, for a while, though."

"Of course." He took a breath. "Then we should probably keep our appointment with the coroner."

They descended into the basement of the hospital—a place chilling in both its temperature and purpose. In a small room, they put on booties, hairnets and paper lab coats.

Dr. Dayani had been apprised of the visit and was awaiting their arrival. Even though cause of death had been apparent at the scene, a full autopsy was still necessary. What hadn't been apparent were the other traumas Elaine Monford had suffered. It had been a difficult autopsy for her.

Wyatt introduced Dave Young, who was unprepared to see such a beautiful woman doing such gruesome work. Griffin had mentioned her and indicated that he was serious in his intentions toward her, even contemplating marriage. Beauty and brains—and empathy. A winning combination, he thought. He was rooting for Ike.

"Will you be arranging for her transfer?" she asked after the introductions were over.

"Yes."

They gathered around the metal table in the middle of the room. A body in a sterile, stainless steel environment often appeared at odds with the same body at a crime scene. Less human, somehow. The stark difference was known to every officer present and, over the years, Dr. Dayani had come to recognize the shift in a viewer's perception.

"I'll begin by saying that she was a previously healthy forty-one-year-old female. The only visible signs of injury that are attributable to the attack are a broken jaw and the abrasions on the back of her head. But I want to warn you that there are some other disturbing injuries that had nothing to do with this attack."

Young knew Elaine's life story, but still he was apprehensive. "I see. Okay," giving her permission to proceed.

When she pulled back the sheet, the first thing to grab their attention was the sewn-up Y incision. Then they saw the scars on her torso. There were sharp intakes of breath.

"Jesus!" Ray said.

"These hypertrophic scars are probably the result of her being burned with cigarettes. There may be more that are invisible to the eye."

Young now wondered if the reason for the loud music was to cover Elaine's screams as she was being tortured.

"Christ! Is there any part of her body without them?" Ray asked, voicing the rage in the room.

"They were only on her torso," she said, giving him a measured look.

"So, always covered up," he said, face grim.

Young then asked the question pressing on their minds, the strain in his voice evident. "Do you know if she was sexually abused?"

"Do you mean at the time of these injuries?"

"Yes."

"We wouldn't be able to ascertain anything at this late stage. However, nothing presents that would indicate anything recent."

"I've seen enough," Young said, his voice thick with emotion, face etched in pain. Elaine had told him that she had been abused, but he hadn't realized the extent of it. He felt a hot rush of anger.

Dayani pulled the sheet back over the body. "Would you prefer to wait a bit before filling in the paperwork?" she asked, her voice soft.

"I'll start now," he said, more sharply than he intended. He turned to Wyatt. "Do you need me for anything else?"

Wyatt shook his head. "No. And thanks very much for coming." Young held out his hand, which Wyatt clasped warmly in both of his. Young understood and gave him a grateful nod.

Ray and Jimmy silently shook his hand and all three left, leaving Young with his tragic responsibilities. And waiting in the future was a visit to an old woman in a care home.

"I don't see any light at the end of the tunnel here, do you?" Wyatt asked, when they had returned to the station.

"The only thing I can think of is reading Monford's reviews in *The Edmonton Times* and *The Bugle* to see if she had really ripped into someone, tipping them over the edge."

"Frankly, it beggars the imagination, Jimmy," Wyatt said, "but if you want to do that, then go ahead."

Ray remained silent. He was as baffled as they were, but remained firm that it was a robbery by a person or persons unknown.

Their discussion broke up on a desultory tone, sinking Wyatt farther into the doldrums. Later, he remembered that he was still in the dark about Young's role in CSIS.

Thirty-two

April 18th

It wasn't yet noon and Jimmy had already read a half-year of reviews on the digitized archives of *The Bayside Bugle*. A few of Elaine Monford's columns had made him wince from time to time, but only one had piqued his interest. He needed to consult Ariel, who was somewhere in the garden taking advantage of a break in the weather. "C'mon Roger. Let's go find Ariel." He got up and began to walk out of the den.

Roger, who had been lying near the mouse on Jimmy's desk, jumped down and ran past him and out the open patio doors. He flopped on the sidewalk and began rolling around from side to side. Molly, perched atop a trellis, dropped down on all fours to a hair's breadth of him. He leaped up and took off, Molly on his tail. They skittered around the corner to the back, where Jimmy expected to find Ariel. All he saw was a bucket filled with weeds and her kneeling pad. And no sign of the cats.

He continued around to the front. But no Ariel. Then he heard Delilah's familiar cackle. Looking across the street, he saw Ariel next to her, smiling broadly and waving at the air with her trowel. She said something that set off Delilah once again. He decided they were having too much fun and turned to go back into the house, but Ariel spotted him.

"Jimmy!" she called to him. "Come on over."

As he approached the two women, he wondered what damage Delilah was doing to the garden. According to Ariel, her macular degeneration had plateaued but she was still unable to differentiate between weeds and flowers, often pulling up both. She was leaning on her small spade, using it for balance. As usual, she was wearing long johns and socks, a muumuu, cardigan sweater and apron. All her clothing was pink, except for her white thermals and the blue and white Toronto Blue Jays cap. She was a die-hard fan.

"Hi there, Sergeant. And if I may say so, you're looking very un-sergeant-like today," she smiled.

"That's because I'm working at home."

"Anything more on that murder?" she asked, eyes glinting.

"Maybe. Maybe not," he grinned.

She tittered and tapped the side of her nose, sprinkling dirt from her gardening gloves onto her face. "Playing your cards close to your chest, eh?" She was hopeful, but knew he wouldn't take the bait.

"How goes your redesign of the town's flower containers?" he said, switching the topic.

"Brilliant! That old battleax is fit to be tied," she laughed.

"Would that 'old battleax' be Vivian Hoffmeyer?"

"One and the same. Wait till she hears what the mayor and I have cooked up for this year. She's going to have a conniption fit."

"Well, I hope it's more of the grasses and drought-resistant flowers," Ariel said. "Is that still in the works, Delilah?"

"Yes. But it's what we are going to put *on* the containers that will have her hair on fire. The mayor is delighted with the idea because it'll raise money."

"Are you going to tell us what that is?" Jimmy asked.

She tossed him a sly grin. "No trades today, I'm afraid."

They laughed. Ariel turned to him. "Were you looking for me when we saw you?"

"Yes."

"Okay. Guess I'll go where I'm needed." She gave Delilah a kiss on the cheek and walked back to the garden with Jimmy. "Oh, look who's waiting for us!" Both cats sat side by side, pretending to be best friends. They immediately separated and zig-zagged in front of their respective servants, nearly tripping them up. "So, what can I do for you?"

"I want you to look at a review that Diane Drake wrote and tell me if it's bad enough to make that person kill her."

She frowned. "Are you seriously considering that as a motive?"

He shrugged. "Don't know. But I need to eliminate it before Ray succeeds in convincing me that it *was* just a foiled robbery."

She glanced at the sky. "Give me a half hour. It's going to rain again, and I want to get at these weeds while the sun is out." There was only a hint of clouds near the horizon, but the weather could change in a heartbeat in Britannia Bay.

Sitting with him at the computer as raindrops dribbled down the window, she read the words: *He should be grateful that there was only a small audience to witness this dog's breakfast.* "Ouch! That's very severe."

"Severe enough to drive someone over the edge?"

She chuckled. "If you knew who she was talking about, you'd deep six that thought. Armand Filiatraut is an effete milquetoast. If you said 'boo' he'd jump a mile. But he would be utterly dejected reading this. It was cruel and totally unnecessary." She paused. "What a witch."

Jimmy had acquired some empathy for Elaine Monford after the autopsy. But he wasn't yet ready to share what he had learned with Ariel, if ever. "Well, I'll just keep looking."

Ariel turned to face him. "Remember when Monique Stepanova went off the rails at the memorial service? There was a review about her string quartet on the day Irina died. Irina and Graham were talking about it that night at choir practice, just before she collapsed."

"I haven't even gotten that far yet." He found the issue for March 1st. "Here it is."

Ariel scrunched close and read along silently with him.

"Jeez," Jimmy's head moved from side-to-side as he scrolled down, reading. After he finished, he turned to Ariel. "Them's fightin' words."

"Perhaps you should interview Monique."

Thirty-three

April 19th

Monique Stepanova had cleared out Irina's suite, selling what she could and donating the rest. Laminate had replaced the carpet, and wood shutters now covered the windows. Once completed, it would be a perfect studio for herself and Grigory. She was looking forward to the convenience, not to mention the money saved now that they would no longer have to shell out for studio space. What she was *not* looking forward to was sorting through Irina's two trunks of memorabilia. The only items she had extracted to date were those she had used for the obituary. But there were shoe boxes full of letters waiting to be read—something to occupy her on a rainy day. A day like today. She was contemplating tackling the job when the doorbell rang.

Peering through the opening, she saw an Asian face. At first glance, she thought he was one of those annoying real estate agents who troll the obituaries checking to see if a house is coming on the market. Then she recognized him, as she had seen him with Ariel Tan at a couple of post-concert receptions given by her string quartet. Was he here collecting for some charity? She opened the door. "Hello Officer Tan. What can I do for you?" Her tone was not warm, but neither was it hostile.

"Hello Mrs. Stepanova. I'm here on police business. I hope I haven't come at a bad time."

"Police business?! Oh. No. I was about to launch into something I've been putting off, so I'm glad for the diversion."

He handed her his card. She noted his rank. "We're investigating the death of Diane Drake and I wondered if I could ask you a few questions."

Curious, she showed him in and directed him to sit on an ornately brocaded sofa, one of the many heavy pieces that Irina brought with her when she moved in with them. Monique had bickered with Grigory about replacing them with something lighter and more modern. He rarely prevailed in their many spats, but in this instance, she had had to back down. He was adamant, which surprised her, because he didn't seem to mind Irina's clothing going to a local theatre company or the Sally Ann. But apparently the family furniture was sacrosanct.

Jimmy sank into the seat and did his best to make himself comfortable.

"I don't know how I can help." She said it so politely that Jimmy wasn't prepared for what came next. "And frankly, I'm not so sure I want to." Her voice had become brittle. "As far as I'm concerned, whoever . . . did away with her, did the music community a favour."

Jimmy had expected an unsympathetic response, but nothing so forthright. Studying her, he saw a striking woman in her forties with silver strands among brown hair, haphazardly fashioned into a French twist. Under her high cheekbones and Roman nose were thin lips and a determined jaw. He decided to be as straightforward as she had been. "We're looking at the possibility that someone in that community might have been driven to kill her."

She threw back her head and laughed, then mocked him with her penetrating green eyes. "Sorry, but I find the idea quite preposterous."

She thought for a moment. "I can imagine a few who figuratively would have driven a stake into her heart—if they could have found one. But literally? No one."

"Not even if their careers were set back or possibly destroyed by something she wrote?"

An ironic smile challenged his hypothesis. "If we gave critics any validation, we would be mad to expose ourselves on the stage."

"But in your mother-in-law's case . . .?" and he left the question hanging.

The sharp angles of Monique's face softened. "I think of her as my mother, Sergeant." She took a moment. "Irina Stepanova was a sensitive soul who loved and protected anyone who was part of her world. In that regard, she was fierce. It not only hurt her terribly when that Drake woman went after a true *artiste*, it made her angry. I'm afraid my mother was one of those persons who *did* take criticism to heart. Not about herself. But for others." She paused. "And *her* heart finally gave out," she added, quietly.

"What about you? You were a target for Drake's poison arrow. I imagine you would have been pretty angry about that last review."

Her head snapped up and her nostrils flared. "You bet I was angry. I wanted to strangle her after I read what she said. Then I considered the source, and let it go."

"Why do you think she wrote that way about serious music?"

"A lack of musical education or curiosity. An inability to see the mathematical nuances, the palette of colours, the emotional depths, the delicacy . . . so many things. It takes dedication to delve into this kind of music, and most people rarely take the time to appreciate anything of value these days. All they want to do is be bombarded by sensations and get instant gratification from *whatever*," she flung out her hand. Just as suddenly as her ardor had sprung to life, it cooled.

Jimmy waited for her to continue, but she had shifted her gaze to the wall behind him as though cutting him from the room. "One last question. A woman was seen running out of the memorial service after you accused Diane Drake of killing your mother-in-law. Did you know her, by any chance?"

Again she waited, seemingly absorbed in what he was saying but wondering if there was a subtext. "First of all, I didn't say she killed Irina. I said she was *responsible* for her death."

Jimmy acknowledged her splitting of hairs with a slight movement of his hand.

She continued. "I did see someone out of the corner of my eye, but I didn't recognize her."

He felt he had learned all he could from her and stood, ready to leave. "Thank you for your time."

"I don't suppose I've shed any light on your investigation—not that I'd lose any sleep over that."

He raised an eyebrow and stared at her for a few seconds. She stared back, then closed the door.

After the detective left, Monique made herself a pot of tea and sighed, turning to her chore. Opening one of the trunks, she smelled the sharp, earthy scent of cedar. Packed among the shoe boxes were strips of the wood, no doubt placed there to keep out musty odors and insects. She placed everything on the floor. Among the boxes were five tied with coloured ribbon and with Cyrillic printing on the tops. It was the same word. She knew enough of the Russian alphabet to figure out what it was. Надин. Nadine. Who was Nadine? There were dates on each box, giving the years. She opened the earliest, dated 2002. And Pandora leapt out.

Thirty-four

By the time Jimmy arrived to the station, he was beginning to think that Ray was right—that it was a robbery that had gone "south," as Delilah had put it. And he said as much to his partner.

"This is how I see it," Ray said, clearly relieved that Jimmy wasn't going to be chasing a wild goose after all. "The perp decides to rob whoever comes out. Maybe someone comes out for a smoke. It doesn't matter if it's one person or a couple. He waits in the bushes near the entrance. Let's say he has a gun or something that looks like a real gun. He's prepared. Then out comes Monford. Alone. He follows her and does the dirty. Takes her wallet and is gone." He slapped his palms on the desk.

Jimmy imagined the scenario, then lifted his hands in a gesture of agreement. "I guess that's the only plausible explanation."

"It is," Ray insisted.

"There are a lot easier ways to steal money, Ray. It seems to be a lot of trouble and planning to hit just one person. And these days cash is rare. So I would've thought he would wait until there were more people. At least that way he would get few more than a few bucks."

Ray was becoming impatient. "Look, Jimmy, anyone who reads *The Bugle* would know there'd be some well-heeled suckers going to that bash. And another thing, this was not an open bar event. People had to buy their own drinks, so the perp knew there would be some cash floating around."

"They may have used credit or debit cards." Then he grasped at the last straw. "And we didn't get anything from all the interviews, did we?"

"Nada," Ray said. "No one saw nuttin'."

Jimmy still wasn't satisfied, but he had struck out with his own theory. "Okay. Let's run it by the chief."

Wyatt wasn't all that happy either. But at least a cocked-up robbery would keep the hounds at bay. If something came up later that would force them to push harder to find Monford's killer, then they would pursue that lead.

Ray grinned broadly. "Now I can go off to Italy with my beautiful women."

Wyatt silently wondered if that was the reason Ray was so eager to put the case to rest. "Well, I guess I'll phone Kittridge and tell him he can run with what we've got."

Kittridge was one more Doubting Thomas. Something about it didn't seem right to him. "How do you feel about this explanation?" he asked Wyatt outright.

"To tell you the truth, Keith, there are things niggling at the back of my mind. I think it's going to keep me awake at night," he confessed.

The editor was surprised at Wyatt's candor. "I'm assuming that's off the record," he said, chuckling.

Wyatt joined him. "You bet your ass."

"Okay. I'll go with the robbery angle. At least the townsfolk won't have to worry about another murder on their doorstep."

Thirty-five

Monique studied the envelope. It had been sent to Irina's former house. The return address was from a Nadine Portman in Edmonton. *I recognize that name. Where have I seen it?* But any immediate search for an answer was overridden by her desire to read the contents. She opened the envelope with care and gingerly unfolded the creased pages. A separate piece of paper fell out. She picked it up. It was a photocopy of a review of the regional Metropolitan Opera auditions in 2002 in Edmonton.

Reading it, Monique felt sick at the play on words of the singer's surname. It was so needlessly cruel. She read on, cringing at the final comment. *"It's true that it wasn't over until the fat lady sang. But at least she had nice hair."* The back-handed compliment was akin to saying that the singer had nothing else going for her. The reporter was Elaine Monford, writing in *The Edmonton Times*. Why would she write such awful words?

She turned to the letter, shot through with humiliation and heartache.

There was a query about her weight. If she lost weight, would she lose her voice? She had heard about Maria Callas losing weight and how it had affected her voice.

Monique read on, plunging into the sorrow of this young girl asking another question. She always threw up before going on stage. How could she stop this?

Monique thought of the courage needed to step on stage, and even more so during the Met Opera auditions. And here was this bitch of a critic putting her down because of her weight. She was angry. She folded the letter, put it back in its envelope with the insert and picked up what she hoped would be a follow-up letter. It was.

Nadine had been grateful for Irina's encouragement and advice. *So, Irina had replied and quickly. Good for her.* Monique began cheering on this young girl, as she picked up a third, then a fourth and fifth missive. By then, she had unwittingly become drawn into a saga that would rock her back on her heels.

Thirty-six

April 22nd

*T*he *Bayside Bugle* arrived on a sunny Saturday morning. Copies were snatched up from doorsteps and the rack at Bayside Foods. Early birds who got their news fix at the Library were upset to see a line-up, only to find that there were the usual three copies available. Impatient, they muttered their annoyance within range of current readers, trying to hurry them along. Some finally gave up, walked to the store and purchased one from a quickly dwindling supply. At least the manager had had the good sense to order extra copies.

There was mixed reaction to the news that Diane Drake, the former Arts Reporter for the paper, had died during a bungled robbery attempt. While some performers or patrons of the arts may have quietly uttered the standard regrets, underlying their sentiments was a feeling of schadenfreude. No doubt others would be less circumspect, throwing off societal constraints and openly celebrating. As for regular readers, they were just relieved that a killer wasn't at large.

Ray, Georgina and Gabriella were together at the breakfast table, an oddity since Gabriella rarely rose before nine on weekends. Along with crumb-covered plates, coffee cups and used utensils, *The Bugle* lay scattered sections on the table.

Gabriella pointed to the paper. "I read one of her reviews once," she announced. "She thought *Farther Out* was a great group. And me and my friends agreed with her."

"My friends and I," Georgina corrected her.

"Oh, not again," she mumbled.

"Yes, again. And I'm going to keep harping at you until you get it right."

"But 'my friends and I' sounds so . . . well, like something one of my teachers would say," she argued.

"Not today's teachers," Ray piped in and put down his cappuccino. "They wouldn't know the difference. No one teaches grammar anymore. And besides, they're hardly older than you. The same generation—the I generation."

Gabriella started laughing. "Dad! It's not the 'I generation.' It's the 'Me generation'."

"Wrong! It's *I* for the *ignorant* generation."

She rolled her eyeballs and tsked. "Honestly. Where do you come up with these things?"

Georgina grinned. "They just roll off his tongue like pearls on a broken string."

"What can I say?" Ray said, smiling goofily and raising his eyebrows twice. "I'm just a genius."

"How do you figure that?" Gabriella challenged him.

Ray picked up the front section of the paper and knocked it a couple of times. "Because *I* was the one who said she was done in by a mugger."

"So, she was just in the wrong place at the wrong time?"

"You got it, sweetie. And just in time for me to go to Italy with my two lovelies here." He rubbed his hands in delight.

Gabriella felt something clutch her heart. She excused herself and left the room. Her parents looked at each other and shrugged.

In the Tan household, Jimmy was brooding, almost ruining the morning for Ariel. Finally deciding she had had enough of his black mood, she went into the garden.

After reading Kittridge's article, Jimmy put down *The Bugle*, and picked up the weekend cryptic. But his mind was not on the clues to the puzzle, but on the clues to the killing. He hadn't been able to bury the idea that Elaine Monford's death was more than a case of happenstance, no matter evidence to the contrary, which was flimsy at best. He couldn't shake his gut feeling. All he could do was wait. Eventually something would arise. He was sure of it. Then he recalled the woman who had been acting a bit odd at the memorial service, and the decal for the car rental company. Maybe there was something there.

He put on a lightweight jacket and went out to find Ariel. "I'm going to get out of your hair for a while."

She knew what that meant, and glared at him. "Jimmy Tan. You need a hobby."

Thirty-seven

As Jimmy pulled into the small parking lot of the airport, a Beechcraft was taking off, heading for Vancouver. He imagined the passengers being mesmerized by the magnificent scenery on the short hop across the strait: majestic mountains, the many islands and inlets, boats of all types and sizes, the occasional ferry and perhaps, breaching Orcas. It was a beautiful, but often bumpy ride.

Chatting to a male employee in coveralls, the agent at Street Fleet Rentals had her back to Jimmy. The man signaled that someone was standing behind her. When she turned, she was as surprised as Jimmy.

"Hi, Mr. Tan!"

"Hi, Madelaine. I didn't know you worked here."

"It's only part time. I'll be leaving for UVic in September."

Ariel had spoken with pride about her star student, who was on her way to begin a Bachelor of Music in Vocal Performance, and with a partial scholarship to help her on her way. "I heard that. Congratulations."

"Thanks. I'm pretty excited about it."

"I'll bet you are. One day you'll be gracing the stages of the Metropolitan Opera."

She blushed.

The man cleared his throat. "I'll push off, Maddy. See you later."

She was puzzled that he was still there. "Oh. Yeah. Okay." A look of annoyance passed across her face. She turned back to Jimmy, lowered her head and whispered, "I wish he wouldn't call me Maddy."

"Tell him that."

"I *have* told him, but he seems incapable of saying 'Madelaine.' I don't know what his problem is."

Jimmy laughed. "Maybe it sounds too sophisticated."

She grinned and shrugged. "Maybe. I don't know. Anyway, what can I do for you, Mr. Tan?"

"Would you mind checking your records to see if a woman rented one of your cars on or about March eighteenth?"

"Sure, no problem." Then her face fell. "Oh, gosh. That was the weekend of Mrs. Stepanova's memorial service." She spoke softly, almost to herself. She sighed, then got busy on the keyboard.

Jimmy waited.

The tapping of the keyboard stopped. She looked up. "I can't find anyone."

He felt his heart drop.

"I mean, I can't find a *person*. The only thing I have is a reservation for Portman Artists' Management." She stopped short, suddenly animated. "Oh! That means a rep company. You know. Like, they represent people in the entertainment industry. Maybe a singer or musician came here for the service." She continued typing. "Here it is. Someone checked out the car on Friday, March eighteenth and returned it on Sunday." She swiveled the monitor around to show Jimmy.

For the first time in days, he felt a prick of hope. Madelaine scrolled to the last page of the application—the photograph of the driver's licence. The person who rented the car that weekend was

Nadine Portman, with an address in Toronto. He felt a frisson of excitement. "Can you make a copy for me?"

"Sure, no worries." She was smiling, sensing a rise in his mood. A few seconds later, she handed him the copy.

"Thanks very much."

"No problem."

After he left, Madelaine logged on to the company's website and looked at the index of artists. There weren't that many, but among them was the name of one of her favourite sopranos. She opened the page. Madelaine wished it had been Nathalie Ellis who had been in Britannia Bay that weekend. Not Nadine Portman.

The police station was quiet. It seemed like weeks since Jimmy had last been there. Robyn Lewitski was manning the front desk and, as usual, had a book in her hands. "What are you reading, Robyn?"

"*His Whole Life,*" she said, holding up the hard cover. It showed the back of a young boy sitting by a pond, alone.

"Is it good?"

"It's wonderful!"

"Would I like it?"

She thought a moment. "I don't know. Maybe. Somehow I think it's more of a woman's book."

He nodded. "I'll mention it to Ariel."

He found Constables Tamsyn Foxcroft and Craig Carpenter in the kitchen, playing cards. There was a pile of chips next to the First Nations woman and very few in front of Carpenter. Everyone at the station knew that he lost to her nine times out of ten. She also beat him handily at rock, paper, scissors.

"She's got you by the short hairs again, I see," he said to Carpenter, whose eyes did a quick flick up at Jimmy, then dropped back to his hand. "Yeah. Bloody Hiawatha," he grumbled.

Foxcroft burst out laughing. There was a time when she would have filed a complaint with the province's Human Rights Tribunal over the racist words. But after working closely with him for two years and realizing he was just a jackass with no agenda, she let his comments roll off her back. They had passed the toleration stage. Now they were on to liking each other. "Cracker boy can't lie down and take a whuppin' from a whoop-whoop. He keeps coming back for more."

Jimmy laughed, and went to his work station, where he began his search of Nadine Portman. The only contact appeared to be the agency's phone number. Being Saturday, he realized it would be closed, but he called and left a message with her answering service.

He scrolled through the pages on the website, noting that she handled opera singers, exclusively. None of their names meant anything to him. In any case, they weren't his focus. He returned to her photograph on the home page and compared it to the shot on her driver's licence. Not all that similar, but that was to be expected. One was professionally taken and the other was a quick flash in the motor vehicle office.

He stared at her face. *So, who are you, Ms. Portman? Why were you at Irina Stepanova's memorial service? And what is your interest in Elaine Monford?*

Thirty-eight

April 23rd, Toronto

On a frigid Sunday morning, Nadine Portman was tucked in at her favourite bakery, indulging in a bagel with cream cheese and home-made raspberry jam, accompanied by a large black coffee and the morning paper. A fierce wind was blowing across Lake Ontario, its intermittent gusts rattling the windows. Her home in the well-established area known as The Beaches was two city blocks away, midway between the lake and the bakery. She wasn't looking forward to the walk. Draining her cup, she donned her winter coat, and took the tray of dishes up to the counter.

"On your way, Nadine?" the woman at the till asked.

"'Fraid so." She hunched her shoulders and acted out a shiver.

"Better you than me," the woman laughed. "See you next Sunday?"

"I'll be here," she said, tugging a thick felt beret over her ears.

Arctic air hit her full in the face as she opened the door. Her old, narrow, three-storey house was situated on an old, narrow tree-lined street, the concrete sidewalk full of cracks and heaves from thick roots and ice. She had spent a good deal of money upgrading the interior and installing storm windows throughout. More than once, she thanked her lucky stars that she had used her father's bequest to purchase it. The timing had been perfect, as the area was being "discovered" and rapidly becoming unaffordable to up-and-comers.

After removing her coat, she headed down the cool hallway and opened a door into a room that faced onto a tiny garden, where planters were sprouting with spring bulbs, some in full bloom, others in various stages of opening. But all had folded in on themselves until they reckoned it was safe to emerge. Adjoining the kitchen, the room was her sanctuary—an office, den and library, with a gas insert fireplace that added an extra touch of warmth on chillier days. Like today.

She slid into her slippers, pulled out her cellphone and sank into her overstuffed chair. Sunday mornings were her chat times with her mother. She scrolled her contact list, hit "Mom" and waited.

But it wasn't her mother who answered. It was Grant. Nadine had had four years to get used to the fact that her mother was co-habiting with a new man. But for whatever reason, Nadine's brain was balking at the idea. It wasn't that she disliked him. It was just that her dad had always been in her corner, rooting for her, and the displacement of him had become a difficult transition. When Grant had been Belle's bridge partner, it was easier for Nadine to accept. Now he was her life partner. Moreover, her mother selling the family home and moving onto rural property with chickens was doubly difficult to absorb. And to top it off, there were their regular motor home trips. She never knew where her mother would be. She found it unsettling. And for some reason, she held him responsible.

"Hi, Grant. Is Mom up?"

"Hello there, Nadine. Absolutely she's up. Up and out on her morning run."

Nadine laughed. "What marathon is she training for now?"

"Well, we're on the road, so just running against herself, I guess. How are you?"

'I'm fine. How's the rebuilding of that school going?"

Grant was one of the many tradesmen who were donating their time to rebuild Fort McMurray. "Slowly but surely, Nadine. It's the rebuilding of the students that's going to be the real challenge. They're suffering from PTSD and—"

But before he could continue, Nadine heard a door open. "Oh, here she is now," Grant said.

There was rustling in the background, then the voice of her mother.

"Hi sweetheart," Belle said, panting.

"Hi, Mom. Should I wait for you to catch your breath?" she teased.

Belle laughed. "No. I'll be okay. Just did a sprint at the end."

"How many kilometers did you do?"

"Just a sec." Her voice turned away from the phone. "Grant, hand me that towel, would you?" A few seconds later she picked up the thread of the conversation. "That's better. Had sweat pouring down the back of my neck. I did the usual ten. So, how are you, darling?"

"Good. Great. Grant said you were on the road. Where are you exactly?"

"San Juan Island, in a gorgeous campsite. One of the few that can take big rigs like this one."

"I still can't believe you drove that motorhome all the way to Vancouver by yourself."

"It's a piece of cake, actually."

Then she heard Grant's voice on the speaker phone. "She was bound and determined to leave before I got back from Fort McMurray. Don't know why she was in such a damned hurry."

"I wanted a leisurely trip without a back-seat driver nattering at me."

"Hah! Leisurely! She drives like a bloody maniac, you know," Grant said.

The two of them laughed. Nadine felt something. What? Jealousy?

The conversation shifted to the weather and then to Nadine's upcoming performance in Santa Fe.

Her mother, excited, cut in. "We've decided to drive down."

"Then you'll be able to come and hear me!"

"Absolutely we will."

It wasn't lost on Nadine that her mother was beginning to use some of Grant's phraseology. Even with that minor prick of irritation, Nadine felt good. Her mother had always been there for her. Like her dad. She had been blessed with the best kind of parents. Loving and supportive. There was only that one dark period when Nadine's peers held more sway over her life. They made her life miserable and she began overeating. Her mother had tried, had used her medical training and contacts in the profession to tackle her eating disorder and get her into programs that purported to be successful. But nothing broke through the psychological barrier enabling her self-destruction. It took a public humiliation and the rescue by Irina Stepanova to put her on the path to recovery.

After their drawn-out goodbyes, Nadine turned to her e-mails and text messages. Nothing urgent. Next she checked her answering machine, jotting down numbers to return. Then came the final caller. And her day went to hell.

"Hello, Ms. Portman. This is Detective Sergeant Jimmy Tan of the Britannia Bay Police Department in British Columbia. Could you please call me at your earliest convenience?" He left his number.

Britannia Bay! She replayed the message. A police detective. What did he want? She felt a prick of panic. why was this detective calling her? Was he connecting her to Diane Drake? How? Going through the events of the day of the memorial service, she remembered the incident in the parking lot. Had he been there? Had he witnessed everything? How had he found her? Had he discovered her secret? Why did he want to talk to her?

The only thing she could do was prepare a story before returning his call. There had to be a plausible explanation for her being at the service and chasing after Drake. She had once read that the best lies contained a kernel of truth. For the remainder of her day, she wove a story until she was satisfied that she had a reasonable facsimile.

Thirty-nine

Back in Britannia Bay

Ray, beady-eyed, watched his daughter step up for Communion. Following closely behind her was Russell Martin. *So, he's a practising Roman Catholic, eh? That's a surprise.* At least Gabriella was smart enough not to glance at him during or after the ritual. Nor did the young man acknowledge her presence.

After the service, Ray continued his scrutiny in the parking lot, earning a poke in the arm from Georgina. "Ray, come off it! You're not even being subtle."

"What?" He tried to look aggrieved.

Georgina rolled her eyes heavenward.

Martin had reached his vehicle and it was only then he dared a quick peek toward the Rossini family. His eyes met those of Gabriella, but there was nothing in the glimpse that suggested they even knew each other, raising Ray's suspicions.

"Did you see that?" he whispered to his wife.

"What? I didn't see anything," she said, her exasperation evident.

"*Exactly.* They're not acting normally."

"With you breathing down their backs? I'm not surprised. You've already read the riot act to him. What's he supposed to do? Come up and greet her like a long, lost friend? Come on, let's go home and have lunch."

Ray kept everyone waiting until Martin's car had rumbled out of the lot and onto the street. There was something about the flames painted on the side of the car that got him hot under the collar.

"Closed until May First" read the sign on the front door of Charterhouse. Jimmy swore under his breath. It was his last stop. He had already crossed off every other B&B and motel open at this time of year. He was weary and the day was wasted. And it was Sunday. A day he should have been spending with Ariel. He dragged himself home where he was certain a thoroughly ticked-off woman would be waiting for him.

Ariel had the lesson plan open before her, frowning. The student who would be arriving tomorrow afternoon was not applying herself. Should she tell her not to waste their time? But she wouldn't say that. She hated to see a potentially gifted singer not realize what a talent she had and where it might lead.

It all began with the high school production of "West Side Story," which Ariel was coaching. As Maria, the girl was not only visually perfect but vocally stunning. Ariel noticed immediately that she had the kind of resonance that would carry to the back row of a concert hall. And with no formal training. Out of all the cast, this girl was the one who had shown incredible promise. Ariel tried to persuade her to develop her talent by taking lessons. When she learned that the girl came from a broken home, with a mother struggling financially, Ariel offered to teach her for free. She soon realized, however, that the girl's focus was on boys, not a future that could lead to Broadway. With a sagging heart, she threw in the towel, not prepared to compete with raging teenage hormones.

She heard Jimmy come through the back door. It was almost five o'clock. Unwilling to let go of the building anger that had been momentarily suspended by her work, she marched into the kitchen, taking in but not taken in by the rueful look on his face. She vented.

"Do you realize that it's dinner time? And, by the way, don't expect any of that," she fairly spat at him. "You've used up the whole weekend with work. Where does it say you have to work on weekends?"

He figured a few seconds of silence would cool down her heat. Remaining calm, he answered, "Because Wyatt told me to use my own time if I wanted to do any follow-up work on this case."

His ruse wasn't successful. Smoke was still coming out of her ears. "And why *are* you still following up? You said yourself that the case had been filed away."

"Because I'm not convinced it should be filed away. There's something there. I can feel it."

She lifted then dropped her shoulders. "Well, I'm not going to question your feelings. They've been right before. But what about *my* feelings? You're mentally absent these days. I could tell you Roger was dead and you wouldn't hear me."

The cat looked up from his bed. Disturbed upon hearing his name among the noise, he rose and padded quickly from the room.

Jimmy dropped his head to hide his smile, but he was stung by the truth of her words. He tried to dig himself out of his hole. "I know. And you're right. But it's just that with the discovery of Nadine Portman, something seems to be leading me somewhere. I don't know what it is. But there's a connection between her and Monford and Irina Stepanova. I have to follow that thread. Even if it seems tenuous."

"Well, what about this Nadine Portman? Who is she?"

"Come with me and I'll show you."

Forty

Jimmy booted up his computer and opened the home page of Portman Artists' Management. On the top right was a photograph of a blue-eyed blond. "This is the woman you and I saw at the memorial service—the one who ran out and looked into Elaine Monford's car." Ariel took a seat next to him.

"Oh." She stretched out the word. "That's interesting. How did you find her?"

"I wanted to tell you yesterday, but you were in a mood. And last night you were at a concert and when you got home you told me you were exhausted and went right to bed. I was gone before you got up this morning. That's why I left you a note."

"Okay. I get it. I'm a slacker who has no time for her husband."

"You got that right."

Ariel directed an elbow at him and missed.

He laughed. "Anyway. To get back to my story. Madelaine, your singing student, works at the airport for Street Fleet. She pulled up the rental agreement for Portman's agency."

"But how did you know to do that?"

"I saw the sticker on the back bumper of the car Portman was driving when she left the parking lot."

Ariel's eyes widened. "God. You never fail to amaze me."

"And make you mad."

"That too." It was her turn to feel chagrined. "But not that often." They exchanged a smile.

He opened the page listing the names of individual artists. "These are the people who have signed up with her."

As he scrolled down the meager list, Ariel stopped him, pointing to a name. "Wait. She manages Nathalie Ellis?"

"It's pronounced Nat-alie?"

"Yes. The *h* is silent."

"And you know who she is?"

"Certainly. She's famous. But I've never heard of any of the others."

"So it's kind of a lopsided list. And a pretty short one, too." He thought about that. "Portman can't be making much money."

"Well, since I already know who Ellis is, why don't we look at the others and see what and where they've been singing? For all I know, they could be performing major roles all over the world." Reading through the curriculum vitae of each singer, they noted that most were in their twenties and not yet performing in the major opera houses outside of North America.

"These singers are working damn hard to survive, picking up roles here and there," Ariel said. "Most companies don't cover their travel and accommodation costs, either. Nathalie Ellis is beyond that scrabble. And you're probably right. She's the only one making money for herself or the agency."

Jimmy clicked the link to her page. "Wow! She's pretty . . . uh . . . dramatic looking." He grinned, knowing what was coming and dodged Ariel's second attempt to jab him.

"Go ahead and say it. She's gorgeous. Everybody knows that."

"It's that come hither look," he teased.

"I found those Harlequin Romances you tried to hide."

"You caught me."

"She does have fabulous hair," Ariel pointed out.

"I wonder when she originally signed with Portman."

"Maybe right after she won the Met Auditions."

"When would that have been?"

"It'll be on their website." She pulled the keyboard and mouse toward her and opened the second monitor. Finding the site for the National Council Auditions, she located the appropriate page. "Here she is with the other finalists."

"So, only nine years ago."

"Obviously her career took off after that." She pointed to the first monitor. "I mean, look at the roles and places where she's sung."

After scanning it, Jimmy said, "Why didn't she move to a bigger agency? Why stay with a small outfit like this one?"

"Probably because the arts world in Canada is so small, almost incestuous. You don't want to ruffle any feathers."

"So Nathalie was loyal to Nadine and Nadine was loyal to Irina for some reason. What do you know about Ellis's private life?"

"Zilch. In fact, no one knows anything about her. And if Portman knows, she's not telling. It seems Ellis suddenly arrived in Toronto, sung one notable role for a small company, blew everyone away, and then disappeared. A couple of years later she gave a spectacular recital by all accounts, and everyone was clamouring to sign her. Opera houses were lining up to offer her plum roles. The funny thing was, there was literally no personal information in her background. It was like she dropped from the sky fully formed." She pointed to the screen. "Citizenship, Canadian. Born, 1984. Period. Usually there would be a ton of stuff. Try someone else."

Jimmy clicked the link to a tenor. Ariel continued: "See what I mean? This guy's got everything here except his high school performance in *Pirates of Penzance*."

After glancing at the list, he returned to Natalie's page. "Just another mystery to add to this investigation," he said. "Maybe Nadine Portman will clear some things up when she returns my call."

"Tell me again why you think she has something to do with Elaine's death."

"Because at the memorial service—if you recall—she ran out and peered into the car driven by Drake, like she was trying to see if she recognized her."

"Oh, yes. I remember that. But she could've just asked the Stepanovs who she was."

Jimmy had already thought of that. "Maybe she didn't want to draw attention to herself."

"It's all very strange, if you ask me. Even a bit sinister."

"Murder *is* sinister."

"So you *do* believe it's murder?"

"Yes. I do. A planned murder."

They sat in silence for a moment or two, reflecting on the implications of his conviction.

"When is she supposed to return your call?"

"I'm hoping tomorrow." He shut off the computer and faced her. "Did you really mean it when you said there was no dinner for me?"

"Nor for me. I got too busy with my *own* work."

He laughed. "Okay. Then let's go to Catalani's." He looked at his watch. "Almost six o'clock. The old folks should have cleared out by now."

Forty-one

April 24ᵗʰ

Wyatt listened as Jimmy pleaded his case. "So, you think there's something about this Portman woman that links her to Monford's murder?"

"I don't know, Chief. It's just a bit off, that's all. I'm curious about why she was showing so much interest in Elaine Monford. After I checked out Street Fleet and got her name, I went around to all the B&Bs and motels, but no one by that name had stayed at any of them. Charterhouse is closed until May first. So I couldn't ask the Abernathys."

Wyatt was rocking back and forth in his chair. He had been doing a lot of that since the squeak had been fixed. The soothing rhythm reminded him of his childhood rocking chair. Maybe he should get one for his den. He was certain it helped with his thinking process. "What's your next move?"

"I'm waiting to hear from her before I consider anything."

Wyatt searched the determined face of his officer. He stopped rocking. "Are you going to run this by Ray?"

Jimmy didn't answer. Ray had already made up his mind that it was a robbery gone wrong. Moreover, he was not focusing on the job, but on his trip to Italy.

Wyatt scratched the back of his neck, and waited. He knew exactly the problem Jimmy was facing and thought he would give him a break. "If I were in your shoes, I would let him go to Italy with nothing on his mind but a holiday. In the meantime, just carry on. If you happen to discover something that *does* give us a clear lead to a suspect, then we *will* have to pull Ray in. Are you okay with that?"

"Yes."

"But on your own time, Jimmy," he cautioned.

"I understand."

For Monique, the letters were a siren song luring her to their lair. She was spellbound by the story unravelling on the pages. Caught up in the drama, she experienced the thrill of excitement that was missing from her life. After her last private student left for the day, she set about making herself a pot of tea, delaying her gratification, a habit since childhood. She believed anticipation heightened an experience.

As she was opening a package of cookies, it came to her where she had seen the name Nadine Portman. With the tea steeping, she went to her desk, opened the bottom drawer and pulled out the Book of Condolences. On the last page she saw the hastily scribbled name and the words written in the Comments section: "We are devastated." So who is "we" and why hadn't Nadine Portman introduced herself?

The sound of Grigory arriving home early set her teeth on edge. She hastily repacked the trunk, keeping her findings to herself—a decision that would threaten her moral compass.

Forty-two

April 28th

Ray had begun singing "Volare" and "That's Amore" from the moment he learned that the financing for the renovations at Catalani's had been approved. He greeted Mary Beth with "*Ciao, bella*" sending the blood rushing up her neck and onto her cheeks. *Grazie, prego,* and *scusi* littered his lexicon.

Novak laughed. "You're about as subtle as a rooster in a hen house."

"So, you're on your way, eh?" McDaniel asked.

"Bags are packed. Leaving tomorrow."

"None too soon for me," Foxcroft said. "You're getting insufferable."

"Hah. *Sei geloso.*"

While she was figuring that one out, McDaniel piped up. "I envy you. I'd love to travel around Italy one day."

"Maybe you and Marina can go there on your honeymoon," Ray teased.

McDaniel shifted uncomfortably in his chair. He and the Media Liaison had been living together for a year now, but no matter how many times he had suggested they get married, she always said she wasn't ready. A marriage she once thought would last forever had ended in a bitter divorce. She was now gun shy, causing no end of grief for McDaniel.

Jimmy chanced a quick look at the constable and saw his downcast face. Other than Novak, he was the only one who knew about Davidova's repeated refusals. Jimmy felt for the big guy, particularly because he knew he would be a loving and devoted husband. He wasn't so sure that Marina would be the same sort of wife. She might be afraid to totally commit a second time. He was thankful that the only baggage he and Ariel had brought to their marriage centered on their families. His own rift had been mended, but they were still waiting for her father to repair the broken bridge with Ariel. The obdurate man just couldn't get past the fact that his only daughter had married a "Chinaman."

His reverie was interrupted by the buzzing of his cellphone. Hoping it was Nadine Portman, he pushed the record button, then answered. After receiving confirmation that it was her, he glanced at Ray, who was busy with paperwork and not paying any attention to his partner. He thanked her for returning his call but refrained from saying her name aloud.

"I'm wondering why you're calling me," she said, sounding more curious than querulous.

"It's to do with your visit to Britannia Bay in March."

"What about it?" Annoyance crept into her voice.

"I understand you were here for the memorial service for Irina Stepanova. You came a fair distance for it. So I was interested in your relationship to her."

There was a long pause. "I'm trying not to sound rude here, but what business is that of yours?" Her tone became prickly.

Okay. You want to play snarky? Jimmy thought. He decided not to pussy-foot around. "We're investigating the manslaughter of a woman, and you were seen looking into her vehicle as she drove off."

Ray, who had begun to pick up the occasional word, was now all ears.

"That woman? She was killed? My God. That's terrible."

"Did you know her?"

"No. As it turns out, I didn't. I got a brief glimpse of her inside the church. But she rushed out so fast that I wasn't sure. I tried to get a better look as she was driving away, but the sun was in my eyes. And she was going too fast."

"Who did you think she was?"

"I thought she was a reporter from Edmonton. But I was wrong."

Jimmy was caught off guard. He hadn't been expecting this. "Are you from Edmonton?"

"Yes."

"What was the reporter's name?"

Jimmy became aware that Ray was listening to his side of the conversation.

"Elaine Monford," she answered.

"How did you know her?"

"I didn't *know* her. I just knew who she was and I was surprised that she might be in Britannia Bay. But, as I said, I was wrong."

"How did you learn you were wrong?"

"When I returned to my B&B, it was corroborated by Mr. and Mrs. Abernathy. I had told them about the brouhaha at the church, and they guessed that the person I saw was most probably Diane Drake. They said she wrote reviews for *The Bayside Bugle*. After they told me her name, I forgot about it."

"You said you were surprised that Elaine Monford would be here. Why?"

"Well, she was the principal reviewer for *The Edmonton Times*. She covered the lion's share of the main musical productions and had made quite a name for herself. She was almost a celebrity in her own right. So, for her to be in such a small town was unthinkable."

"But didn't you make a connection between the fact that both women wrote reviews?"

"I just thought it was a coincidence. That's all."

Jimmy let that pass. Perhaps coincidences didn't arouse the same suspicion in the general public as they did for cops.

"Wait," she continued. "Are you saying that the woman I saw *was* Elaine Monford?"

"Yes."

"But that's astonishing. Why would she be in Britannia Bay? And why was she murdered?"

"At this point, it appears someone was trying to rob her and mistakenly killed her." He slid by her first question.

"Oh, how awful."

He pressed on. "By the way, how did you know Irina Stepanova?"

"She's . . . she had been to Toronto many times. We met through a mutual friend. She sent a couple of very good singers to me. I was struggling to get my agency going and finding it hard to sign anyone. She got the ball rolling. Needless to say, I was very grateful to her."

Jimmy waited. But in this case, his silence didn't elicit another word from her. "Well, thank you very much for clearing this up." After the goodbyes were said, Jimmy shut off his recorder.

Ray stood, shaking his head back and forth, his mouth in a grim line. "What the hell was all that about?"

"Tying up loose ends, Ray."

"You're like a bloody dog with a bone, you know that?" He glared at Jimmy. "And who is this woman you were talking to, and what has she got to do with this case?"

"She had shown a lot of interest in Diane Drake at the memorial service. She thought Drake might be Elaine Monford. But the

Abernathys disabused her of that. So, she was none the wiser at that point. As it turns out, however, she *did* know her. But in Edmonton, where she used to live. I wanted to wring everything out of her I could. Her interest was bugging me. And those coincidences still bug me."

Ray contained his irritation by drawing in a deep breath and blowing it out in one long, slow stream of air. "I thought we had closed this case."

"It's not closed, Ray, and you know it. It won't be closed until we've found who did it. So, as far as *I'm* concerned, at this point it's a cold case."

"Hmph. Well, that's something, at least."

"Well, maybe more like warm," Jimmy needled him.

Ray threw up his hands. "Oh, for fuck's sake!" Then he chuckled. "So, can I go to Italy and not worry that you're gonna come up with another cockamamie idea while I'm gone?"

"Yeah. Yeah." He picked up his cellphone and waved it at Ray. "But I'm going to play this for the chief." He still wasn't ready to go along just to get along.

Wyatt mulled over what he had heard in the recorded conversation. "Those ties linking Portman with Monford and Stepanova may be tenuous but they're a bit sticky, too."

"That's what I think. If it's okay with you, I'd like to try to find out more about her."

"Fine, but don't let it occupy too much of your time, Jimmy. This may be one of those cases that lies in the freezer for years."

Forty-three

Monday, May 1st

Enjoying the breakfast that their cook had placed before them, Clive and Daphne Abernathy were thankful to be back at Charterhouse after ten days in Billericay, England. They had planned on touring around Essex, their old home county. But the rain and poor transportation had skewed all their plans. Not only that, their encroaching old age had defeated them. They simply hadn't the energy to explore farther afield than Chelmsford. Their little village of Britannia Bay had never been so welcoming. Calvin's exuberant displays and squawks added to their grateful homecoming. And today Heritage Gardens was being opened for the season. Abernathy was eager to get back to exercising his role as President.

Someone rang the front door chimes, but they left it for their housekeeper to answer. A moment later, she came into the kitchen. "There's a police officer here to see you, Mr. Abernathy."

He, his wife, and the cook all looked up, surprised.

"*Gracious!* At *this* hour?" He gave a quick exhale of irritation. "Show him into the library, Louise, and tell him we'll be right there." Vexed at having to leave his food, he threw down his napkin. "Bryony, would you mind putting our plates in the warming oven?" Then he shot a look at Daphne whose pale eyes were wide with curiosity. "Come on, pet. Let's see what he wants."

Jimmy was standing with his back to them, taking in the many and varied volumes lining the bookcases. He was about to reach for *The Meditations of Marcus Aurelius* when he heard their footsteps.

"Good morning," Abernathy greeted him. "I see we meet again." His tone was as neutral as he could manage.

"Good morning. I apologize for coming so early. I hope I haven't interrupted your breakfast." He had smelled bacon and coffee upon entering the house.

"We were just finishing up," Abernathy lied through a tight smile. "What is of such importance that it brings you to our establishment at this hour?"

"I wanted to confirm that you had a certain guest here the weekend of March eighteenth. Her name was Natalie Portman."

"Oh yes. Miss Portman." He looked up and away as he recalled her. "Lovely woman."

"She had the most *gorgeous* hair," Daphne said.

Her husband ignored her. Concern crept into his voice. "I hope nothing has happened to her."

"No. It's just a general inquiry."

"I see. Well, she stayed two nights. She was here for the memorial service for Madam Stepanova."

"By any chance did she discuss a possible relationship with her?"

Abernathy hesitated as he recalled the conversation they had had after the service. "No. She just brought up the fact that there had been a rather *ugly* scene with Diane Drake afterward. That led to a discussion about the reporter."

"Did she seem overly curious about Miss Drake?"

"No," he said.

"Well, actually, she did," Daphne interjected.

Abernathy was surprised at her interruption and a slight flash of annoyance crossed his face.

"How so?" Jimmy asked.

"We had mentioned that her reviews were unkind on many occasions, and Clive brought out some old issues of *The Bugle* for her to read," Daphne offered.

Abernathy recovered and nodded his head. "Yes. That's right. I remember now. She took a few copies to her room, in fact."

"Did she leave them behind when she checked out?"

"As far as I know. But you would have to ask our housekeeper. Mind you, that was over a month ago, so she may not remember. Would you like us to call her in?"

"No. It isn't necessary. I think I have everything I need. Thank you very much." Jimmy stood, signaling the end of his visit.

"You're welcome."

As Jimmy passed by Calvin, the bird let out a squawk, causing him to jerk out of the way. He caught the Abernathys covering their smiles.

When he was gone, the couple laughed out loud. "Oh, that was *delicious!*" They returned to their warmed-over breakfasts and ruminated about the reasons for the officer's visit, an activity that would occupy them until such time as other morsels of gossip popped up to feed their appetites.

Something that Jimmy had heard at Charterhouse was stuck in the back of his brain, and he couldn't dislodge it. Any attempts would only make it worse. He had to free his mind and let his subconscious work in peace. There was only one place where that would happen. "I'm going to the do-jo," he told Ariel that evening.

Ariel started singing, "Going to a go-go," and was dancing around the kitchen when Jimmy left just as Lana arrived.

"What are you laughing at?" she asked him.

"My crazy wife." He gestured behind him with his thumb, then gave her a hug. "Have a great time."

"You can bet on it." She stepped into the kitchen, and joined in the singing, adding the "oh, oh" to the refrain. They stopped, high-fived and laughed.

"I love that song," Ariel said.

"Me too." Lana had long ago learned that her friend appreciated a variety of musical genres.

"I seem to have worked up a thirst. What about you? Would you like something to drink?"

Lana stayed standing. "Actually, no booze tonight, Ariel. I want a nice, normal sleep. It's going to be hard enough having to use an alarm clock. It usually means I'm awake all night."

"I can give you a wake-up call, you know."

"Well. Okay. But it's six o'clock."

"We'll be up by then."

"Okay."

"Are you sure you don't want a ride to the airport?"

"Street Fleet are picking me up."

"If they aren't here by the time you're ready to leave, call me."

"Okay. That's a deal."

"I'll miss you. I know you'll be having a great time, but send e-mails and photos when you think of it."

"I will."

They hugged, and said their goodbyes.

A sense of loneliness swept over Ariel. She reached down and picked up her cat. "Come on, Molly. Keep me company." Molly stuck her nose in Ariel's armpit and purred.

Forty-four

May 15th

Delilah sat on her walker while she and Mayor Verhagen watched the landscaper overseeing final touches to the installation in the town square. While she was happy enough that the Council had agreed to honour Irina Stepanova with a commemorative fountain, she was tickled pink that her suggestion for its placement had been given a green light. It seemed a fitting spot, nestled into a small garden in front of the cultural centre.

"It looks lovely, don't you think?" she asked Verhagen.

"It certainly does." His mind was already counting the coins that would be tossed in the water.

"Just hope the birds don't decide to poop in it. You know, they poop where they drink *and* bathe." She smirked. "It's disgusting, if you ask me. Pretty creatures with dirty habits."

The corners of Verhagen's mouth turned down. "Why didn't anyone ever mention this?"

She shrugged. "I did. But I was drowned out by the dunces you have sitting around that table."

He did a quick memory check of the Council members and had to agree that most of them were one sandwich short of a picnic. "Oh, well. The maintenance workers will take care of that." And *he* had to take care that they didn't pocket the coins. They were for the city coffers until the "dunces" could decide which charity would get the benefit. Thinking of that, he turned to her. "We brought in quite a tidy sum for those plaques, Delilah."

"I knew you would. Who wouldn't love having their names associated with flowers?" Then she thought of Vivian Hoffmeyer. *Too bad there wasn't a container for cactuses. Or is that cacti?* "I suppose you're going to make a speech when the fountain's unveiled, eh?"

"Of *course* I am," he huffed. Then stupidly asked, "Why?"

"Because people hate speeches. Long speeches. You need to keep it simple," and caught herself before saying *stupid*. "Let the family speak. It will be their day."

He looked down at her. "In actual fact, Delilah, it will be Victoria's Day," he said, attempting a joke on the upcoming holiday.

She grinned weakly. *Lord, give me strength.*

He had already prepared what he was going to say. But her words gave him pause. People *would* appreciate something shorter. He didn't want to seem to be stealing the spotlight. Not that he ever had. Or ever could. "Perhaps you're right. Less is more." He had heard the same words from his wife. Another wise woman. That thought in mind, he thanked her and left to do a rewrite.

Delilah smiled to herself. *He is so easy.*

Unlike the town, which was bustling with the first seasonal rush of tourists, the police station had taken on a morgue-like atmosphere. Ray's absence had left behind a black hole sucking all the life out of the squad room.

With nothing more than a few scattered petty crimes to handle, Jimmy had had ample time to check into Nadine Portman's skeletal background in Edmonton and to search old issues of *The Edmonton Times* for Elaine Monford's reviews. He had retrieved her case file and been looking for something more as a motive for her murder. It was now time to follow through on a plan he had been mulling over. He picked up his cellphone and made a call.

Wyatt looked up as Jimmy tapped on the open door. "C'mon in, Tan. What do you need?" he asked, knowing no one knocked on his door for nothing.

"Can I have a word?"

"Sit yourself down." He sharp-eyed Jimmy and waited.

Jimmy plunged in. "I've been looking at the Monford file again."

Wyatt felt a tiny smile growing at the corners of his mouth and quashed it by pursing his lips. It was inevitable that Tan would pick at this investigation until it unravelled to reveal something underneath the surface. The surprise was that it had taken this long.

"Okay," Wyatt said noncommittally.

"I want to go to Edmonton, Chief. The editor of the paper Elaine worked on has been there for years. I've just spoken to him and given him some background on our case. But I want to talk to him one-on-one. Get a feel for his impressions. I also want to check on Nadine Portman's background there. I think there's some kind of link, particularly because her agency manages opera singers. It's too coincidental. All of it."

Wyatt watched as Jimmy worked himself up, a rarity for the normally unflappable cop. "But it's a pretty flimsy connection, don't you think?"

Jimmy shrugged. In a way, Wyatt was right. "Elaine had secrets. So does Nadine Portman," was all he could say.

"And you think digging around might unearth something useful?" Rather than wait for a reply, Wyatt began tapping the computer keyboard, bringing up a spreadsheet. After a moment, he turned to Jimmy. "You know we don't have a budget for this kind of thing, Tan."

Jimmy heard an opening. "I know. I'll pay for it myself."

Wyatt raised his eyebrows. "Just a second, then." He pulled up another document. "Looks like you'll have to wait until after the Victoria Day weekend when Atkins returns from his holidays. He's the only other D.S. now that Ray's gone." Then he tossed a slider at Jimmy. "I'm assuming you're going to dip into your vacation time to do this." It was more a statement than a question.

Jimmy knew his boss was being a bit hard-nosed about his request, but he was prepared to accept the limits placed on him. Jimmy smiled. "No problem. Thanks, Chief."

Wyatt smiled. "You're one for the books, Tan. I'll give you that. Now get out of here."

Roger had picked up on the crackle of energy emitting from his master, winding his tail around Jimmy's legs, purring while his food was being prepared. Then, as his bowl was being placed on the floor, he rubbed his cheek against Jimmy's hand, nearly upending his dinner.

Jimmy laughed and gave him a pat on his head. "You're as happy as I am, aren't you, big boy?"

Ariel strolled into the kitchen. "Yeah. It's catching. Like Santa arriving early."

"It feels good to get some movement on the case. Now I just have to figure out where Nadine fits in with Elaine's murder. If at all." Yet, the words that hadn't come unstuck at the do-jo kept nudging against his subconscious. Later on, he stared once again at Nadine's picture as though it might solve the riddle. There was an instant when there was a flicker of something, but then Ariel called him, and the suggestion in her voice had him quickly shutting down the computer and heading for bed.

Forty-five

May 22nd, Victoria Day Holiday

It would take more than a commemorative fountain to honour Irina Stepanova, Monique thought, as she took her seat near the podium in the town square. But Grigory told her that the tribute was a nice gesture, and she supposed he was right. Unlike her, he always saw the bright side of things. She put her cynical *conception du monde* down to her Gallic heritage.

As a few more stragglers gathered around, she noticed Ariel Tan standing at the back with her detective husband. He had been so sober, so earnest in his desire to find Monford's killer. And now, in an exchange of letters, she had found the means to help him. But the question was, did she want to?

Mayor Verhagen stepped behind a lectern and searched the tiny knot of people for the press photographer. Spotting him, he removed the speech from his pocket, tested the microphone and began his address. Following the advice of Delilah and his wife, he had kept his words to a minimum, and was rewarded with a nice hand. *That should serve me in good stead come the next election.* He smiled, then relinquished his place to Grigory Stepanov.

Monique inspected her husband of twenty-eight years. He hadn't aged that well. Or was it just that he was not robust, spending all his time indoors under artificial lighting? He never went outside. Unlike her. In decent weather, she took long walks along the quay. Those perambulations allowed her mind to either wander or focus. For the past month, it had been consumed with the relationship between Irina and Nadine. Monique almost resented the fact that Irina hadn't shared this amazing story with her. They had been close. Or so she thought.

As each letter opened on another chapter in Nadine's life, Monique realized how dull her own life had been. The only excitement had been during trips to Europe, thanks to grants from the Canadian Council for the Arts. So often, she wished she could remain in whatever foreign city where they were performing. Any one of them would have offered more than what was available in Canada. Certainly in Britannia Bay. She fantasized about being single again. Free to live a different life. Like Nadine.

And then there was her marriage. If she could call it that. It was more like a musical arrangement with no discordant notes, but no dizzying riffs either. Only bars and bars of the same bland *motif*. No hidden subtext.

Now she was hiding something from the man speaking to the small but appreciative audience. She would give him that. He was always good at engaging an audience. He could speak off the cuff at concerts, never needing notes about intricate histories of a composer or composition. And his quick wit always added a less formal and human touch to his orations. He was easy, approachable. People always wanted to chat with him after a performance.

She didn't have that facility. Conversations for her were difficult. Hugs were out of the question. Alien. She had only managed these things with her children when they were toddlers. And with Irina. But that was all down to Irina, who connected with people. Monique viscerally felt Irina's deep empathy for Nadine. She gave of herself. Monique could never do that. She believed if she gave, there would be less available for herself.

Her thoughts were interrupted by applause. She hadn't heard a word. But she suddenly realized she needed to join her husband at the podium. As she smiled and nodded, her eyes strayed to the Tans. Jimmy locked on to Monique's gaze and held it. For a moment she was frozen. Then Grigory took her arm and they moved forward to thank the mayor. With the short ceremony over and pictures taken, they turned to leave. Monique looked back. The detective was watching her. Why?

In Toronto, Nadine read the tribute article on *The Bayside Bugle's* website. Ever since her mother had confirmed that Elaine Monford had last written a column for *The Edmonton Times* two years previous, Nadine had been reading the on-line editions of the paper, convinced now that Drake was Monford. She knew it was a ridiculous thing to do, but she couldn't seem to help herself. Then came the shock of Drake's death, attributed to a robbery.

She stared at the picture of the Stepanovs with the mayor. A fountain! A fountain to honour one of the finest singers of her day. What a farce!

She closed the site and settled back in her chair, allowing memories of Irina and her friend Loretta Alba, and the vocal coach *straordinario* Fabio di Fiore, to flow through her mind. She laughed out loud thinking of the mystery they had cooked up. What a hoot it had been. And they had pulled it off.

Now, here she was. Famous but fraught. Thank God she had the upcoming production of *La Favorita* in Santa Fe to take her mind off Britannia Bay. Singing was the only remedy for an intrusive world.

Forty-six

Ariel was clearing the plates from the table and handing them to Jimmy, who was stacking them in the dishwasher. Delilah watched the pair of them in their practiced routine and thought about how things had changed. In her day, men didn't lift a finger to help around the house. Now they pitched in, if they knew what was good for them. Women were busy, holding down jobs, raising children, shopping, cooking and cleaning. Today they parceled out some of that work to their partners. Delilah thought it made for a healthier relationship; more balanced.

"Are you going down to watch the fireworks?" she asked them.

"Not this year. We've had our fill of them, and it stays light for so long that it's too late for us," Ariel said.

"Yeah. We old fogies have to be in bed by ten o'clock," Jimmy added.

Delilah chuckled. "Old fogies. Huh! Old is a dirty three-letter word."

"So you keep telling us, Lilah," Ariel smiled. "So when is old *old*?"

She took a moment to think about that. "When nothing strikes you funny anymore. I know old people in their twenties. Might as well be dead, as far as I'm concerned. Never laugh. Their mouths are as tight as their butts."

Jimmy almost dropped a plate. Ariel burst out laughing.

"Pardon my French," Delilah added, eyes twinkling.

"Honestly, you naughty girl. You're one for the books," Ariel said.

"Yes. And in the Good Book, too. Delilah was a naughty woman. I could never understand why my mother called me Delilah. Maybe she had an inkling of what kind of person I'd turn out to be."

Ariel came over and put her hands on Delilah's shoulders. "You may be a bit naughty, Lilah, but you're a gem—full of sparkle. And you're a lovely, lovely woman. Don't you ever forget it."

"Oh, go on with you," she said, her voice cracking. She abruptly stood. "I'd better get home before Tabitha takes another chunk out of my sofa."

"Thank you for keeping us company," Jimmy gave her a quick hug.

"And thank you for the dinner. It was delicious, as usual."

Ariel retrieved a covered bowl and held it out to her. "I'm glad you liked it because here's more for you for tomorrow night."

"Now who's the gem?" She put the container in her walker basket. Jimmy opened the door and saw her out. He waited until she had gone into the house and shut her door.

"I hope we never lose our ability to laugh at things," Ariel mused.

Jimmy thought about his work. "Sometimes it's hard. I'm lucky to have you. You always get me through the dark times."

He put his arms around her, holding her. They rocked side-to-side. When they broke apart, he looked at her. "Can I ask you something about today?"

She sat down. "What?"

"It's about Monique Stepanova."

Ariel lifted her eyebrows. "Gosh. What about her?"

"She was miles away. I was watching her and she was just not there. You would have thought that she would be concentrating on everything her husband was saying. It was an important day and he said some nice things about Irina."

"Maybe it's just that she'd already heard it. Maybe he practiced in front of her. Or maybe she *has* heard it all before. You know? How wonderful her mother-in-law was and all the things she had done for the community. Et cetera. Et cetera. Maybe her mind just wandered. Or perhaps she was thinking her own private thoughts about Irina."

Jimmy listened and after Ariel finished, he nodded. "You're probably right. It's just that I find her so . . . I don't know. So cold."

"She does have that reputation. Maybe all of her warmth is showered on her students. I know they adore her."

"I'd like to see some proof of that."

"Well, in June I'm going to her year-end student recital. Maybe you could come along and see it first-hand."

He put up both his hands. "No thanks. Include me out," he laughed.

"Can we change the subject? It's your last night home for a couple of days. Let's dwell on us."

"I'm all in on that, baby."

Forty-seven

Edmonton, May 25th

It was an endless horizon. The only break in the skyline was a vast industrial complex whose sole *raison d'etre* was to service the oil industry throughout the province. The odd pumpjack dotted the landscape, extracting what remained of the petroleum that had been discovered in Leduc some seventy years before—an event that almost didn't happen. After drilling 133 dry holes and pouring millions of dollars into the exploration effort, Imperial Oil was ready to give up. This was their last chance. Finally, on the afternoon of February 13th, 1947, a stream of clear, light crude burst out through the gush of mud. And Alberta was changed forever.

In planning his trip, Jimmy had briefly read the history of the area. Now his mind was on other stories. He recalled his conversation with Ariel about Nathalie Ellis and her biography, written by a minimalist.

"She's kind of like Andy Warhol," she said.

"How do you mean?"

"Well, when he was asked where he was born, sometimes he would say one state, and then another time, he would say it was a different state. It created this mysterious aura that lured in a lot of people. And that's the same with Nathalie."

"He wouldn't have been so cavalier today with all the search capabilities at our fingertips. Literally."

"But no one's found out anything about her," she argued.

"Not yet."

His thoughts turned to other inventions and reinventions—his own life story. The nebulous relationship to his aunt, Tan Teck. His falsified birth certificate. Wrought through with subterfuge and bribery, his identity was a ticking bomb. At any moment, someone in Malaysia could decide he or she wanted more in order not to divulge Jimmy's true origins. So far, whatever money had been shelled out by his aunt had held that prospect in abeyance. Would there come a time when the blackmail would end? Probably when the last individual with the knowledge died. Right now that would be his younger half-brother—a spoiled, witless, disaffected man-child. Jimmy often wished for an untimely accident to cause his early demise. But he bit back the thought, thinking of the Golden Rule. Not to mention karma.

Nearing the city, he turned on the GPS to find his hotel. A few minutes later he pulled up to the front of the Fairmont Hotel Macdonald. These were luxurious accommodations that not many police officers could afford. But not many police officers had fathers who had been worth millions. And with Tan Teck's urging, he had finally dipped into his inheritance in order to pay for it.

A valet instantly approached his rental car and saw to its parking while a bellman unloaded Jimmy's leather satchel and laptop case and waited until he had signed in. After a quick elevator ride, they entered a large room facing the North Saskatchewan River, its clear waters flowing from the Columbia Icefield. At that moment, a large canoe holding a dozen or so paddlers was just passing out of sight.

"Wow! This looks like a travel brochure."

"Yeah. It's pretty nice, all right. Even though there aren't that many floors, the hotel is high enough on the ridge to provide a great view." He then ran through the list of amenities, and then added that a concierge was available 24/7 should he need anything extra.

Jimmy wasn't sure what he meant by the last comment, but he saw no suggestive look on his face. He tipped him, and after he left, the first thing Jimmy did was open a window, something rare in most hotels. The air was cool and refreshing coming off the river. There were sounds of cutlery and crystal coming up from the terrace, where diners were enjoying a late *al fresco* lunch. He realized that he was hungry. The bellman had mentioned a room that served light meals from six in the morning until midnight. As soon as he unpacked, he would go downstairs to eat.

After putting away his few items, he connected his laptop and printer behind a writing desk. Checking his cellphone, he saw one call from Ariel and another he recognized as being from Henry Pristupa, the editor of *The Edmonton Times*. He called him first.

"Pristupa here." The voice suggested energy.

"Hello, Mr. Pristupa. This is Jimmy Tan. I've just arrived."

"Oh, here already? Good. Where are you staying?"

Jimmy was almost embarrassed to tell him and when he did, he was met with silence, followed by a guffaw. "Are you Canada's version of Inspector Thomas Lynley, by any chance?"

The reference to the fictional detective reminded him of how he and Ariel had enjoyed the television series. "I'm just about to have lunch downstairs. But I could come by after that, if it's convenient, that is."

"Lunch. What's that?" he chuckled.

Sensing an opportunity, Jimmy seized it. "Would you like to join me?"

"That sounds like a great idea. Just a second." Jimmy heard a muffled conversation, then Pristupa asked, "What dining room?"

"The Harvest Room."

"Okay. I'm just a fifteen minute walk from there."

"I'll leave my name with the maître d'," he said, although he doubted there would be more than one lone Asian male sitting at an empty table. He returned Ariel's call, updating her on the trip and the hotel. "I wish you were here. The room is too nice not to share. And the bed is the size of a tennis court."

"So, does that mean you're going to hire a playmate to have a few sets with?"

"Get serious. Can you see me with a call girl?"

"Well, maybe one of those educated types that international big shots always seem to get trapped with."

"I'd rather read a book."

"As long as it's not *Fifty Shades of Grey.*"

"You mean that book about hair stylists?"

"Oh, ha ha."

"I have to go. I'm meeting the editor of the paper downstairs for lunch. I'll call you tonight."

"Just one more thing. I got an e-mail from Lana this morning. She's in Pesaro with the Rossinis and having a terrific time. She's leaving for Paris tomorrow."

"Don't worry, Ariel. You'll get back there, and this time you'll have me to show around."

"If we don't hurry up, we'll be strolling the Champs Elysees with our walkers. Now, go enjoy your lunch."

"Yes ma'am. Give Roger a kiss from me." He heard her snickering as he ended the call.

In the dining room, Jimmy perused the menu and saw several choices that all seemed to centre on beef. Ariel had done her best to wean him off red meat, but real hunger aroused an atavistic craving in him. Right now the Angus beef burger medium rare would assuage that. And with fries. And a beer. Jimmy gave the waiter his order but told him to hold off until his guest arrived. He showed him his keycard and said that the entire bill should be charged to his room. As the waiter turned away, Henry Pristupa walked in and caught his attention.

"Yes, sir?"

"Could you bring me a Crafty Bastard?"

"Right away." He turned to Jimmy. "Are you going with the Stella Artois?"

Jimmy grinned. "Was that Crafty Bastard a person or a beer?"

The waiter chuckled. "Yes, a lager."

"I'll try that."

"Very good, sir." He turned to Pristupa. "I'll bring a menu."

Jimmy sized up the man standing beside the table. He looked to be in his late sixties; a bit on the short side, and except for a slight paunch, appeared to have a muscular body. He was totally bald, but had a thick and bristly salt-and-pepper moustache. Eyes like hard, dark marbles were set deep between bushy white eyebrows and prominent bags. The top of his head and his forearms below his short-sleeved shirt were brown, as though he spent a lot of time outdoors.

Before sitting, he reached down and shook Jimmy's hand. "Nice to meet you." His hands were rough. He settled into the chair. "Warmer than usual out there. A cool beer will hit the spot." He glanced around, drumming lightly on the table top as he did. "Nice digs. Have you ordered yet?"

"Yes."

"What're you having?"

"A burger."

"Good choice. I'll have the same. You having fries, too?"

"Yes."

"You live dangerously."

The waiter brought over the beers in chilled glasses and took out the menu tucked under his arm.

"I don't need that after all," Pristupa said, "I'm going to have the burger with fries, too."

"How would you like it cooked?"

"You mean we have a choice? Don't you have to cook it until it looks like a lump of coal? Have to kill all of that e-coli, you know." He squinted at the waiter.

"No sir. No chance of that. The hotel is very particular about our suppliers, and our health and safety standards." The man was parroting what he had been trained to say.

"I know. I'm just pulling your chain. Hotels can't risk getting sued. Then I'll have it charred on the outside and pink on the inside. And throw in some onion rings."

"Now who's living dangerously," Jimmy said, as the waiter left.

"Touché." He picked up his glass. "To the good life," he said.

"I'll drink to that."

They both took long draughts, after which Jimmy remarked on how good it was.

"You bet it is. The only other place it's available in town is at The Craft Beer Market. I would have suggested meeting there, but it's too damned noisy. Can't carry on a conversation, and for me that's deadly because I don't do well in ambient noise. Have to read lips. Could really screw up a news story if the guy was saying looker and I heard hooker."

"I'll be sure to enunciate clearly."

They chatted, making small talk until the waiter came with their platters of food. Jimmy gawked. "This burger's as big as a frisbee."

"Yeah. Try enunciating around that," Pristupa chuckled.

For Jimmy, this was the last of the levity. During the meal, he learned more than he cared to know about the problems surrounding the oil sands. "And be careful not to say tar sands around here. That's not what they are, anyway," Pristupa advised him. Then went on to explain the difference. Next came a rant against the Prime Minister, Justin Trudeau. "Naïve kid. Should never have been elected. Look what he's doing to Alberta. Right off the bat. Just like his dad. Killing this province for whatever reason. Bunch of French-Canadian elitists." And he went off on another tangent.

By the time they had finished eating, Jimmy's teeth were ready to bleed. He hadn't counted on a harangue about politics. Then he recalled Wyatt's words: "You're going to a region of the country where there are a lot of grievances, Jimmy. Be careful you don't put a foot wrong."

Forty-eight

After coffee was poured, Pristupa finally wound down on what had to be his number one topic. "Well, now that I've given you an earful on where Alberta stands in this so-called confederation, let's talk about the reason you're here." He took a last sip of his beer. "First of all, though, you should know that I know why Elaine was in your town."

Pristupa's revelation stunned Jimmy. "You didn't mention that when he talked." There was an undertone of mild anger in his words, which wasn't missed by the editor.

"No. I did not. And I don't apologize for it. I don't trust any communication that isn't face-to-face, and sometimes not even then."

Jimmy thought of the on-going tug-of-war between the police and the press. There was certainly plenty of evidence for it. And these days, the press seemed to be pulling with the weight of the public behind them.

With no further explanation, Pristupa carried on. "Now, with that out of the way, I take it that you think there's something else in her background that led to her murder. You don't believe it was a professional hit by one of Jabril Barre's thugs or a botched robbery."

"Definitely not the first. As for the second, there are some doubts about it."

"And the daughter-in-law blames Elaine for causing missus Stepanova's death?"

"Yes."

"So am I right—that you're looking at revenge from an aggrieved performer? Someone who hated Elaine Monford enough to kill her?" He frowned, reflecting his skepticism.

Jimmy shook his head and lifted his palms. "It's a stretch but I don't know where else to look."

The detective's defeatism had Pristupa searching for some encouragement. "Well, you could be right. A famous conductor once said to a female cellist, 'Madam, you have between your legs an instrument capable of giving pleasure to thousands and all you can do is scratch it.' I think if I'd been her, I would've bashed him over the head with the cello."

Jimmy laughed, grateful for the man's empathy. "Did you ever have any concerns for Elaine's safety?" he asked, after a pause.

"Not really. But we had to ask her to tone down her copy on a number of occasions because some of it was bordering on libel. Or at least legal trouble of one sort or another. She had a way with words and liked to show it. She was damned clever. But she could be cutting. If this had been the early 20th century, she could've been writing for a broadsheet in Toronto or Montreal—maybe even some large American city."

"She was that good?"

"She was that good."

Jimmy thought of Elaine, no doubt bitter over her banishment to a one-horse town, writing for some two-bit tri-weekly.

The waiter came by with a fresh carafe of coffee and refilled their cups. After they both took sips, Pristupa asked Jimmy the obvious question. "But why look here, when your killer was more than likely someone from your area? No one's going to go there and murder her.

Especially after she's been gone a couple of years."

"We questioned everyone who might have had a grievance against her and couldn't find anyone suspicious enough to consider." He paused. "But there was an occurrence that piqued my curiosity. It involved a person who was at the memorial service. Someone who comes from Edmonton. Someone who knew who Elaine was."

Pristupa's eyes gleamed. "You don't say."

Without mentioning her name, Jimmy began relating the details about Nadine Portman's odd behaviour, when Pristupa cut in.

"There was an incident about . . . well, over ten years ago, or so. I can't remember exactly when. But there'll be something in the archives about it. Anyway, a man barged in raising holy hell and threatening to sue us for something Elaine had written about his daughter. He probably would've strangled her if she had been there. Thank God she wasn't. Both for him and for her."

Jimmy, nerves tingling, tossed his napkin on the table and got up. "Let's go find that 'something,' in your records."

"What about the bill?"

"It's covered," he said quickly, anxious to leave.

Pristupa wasn't going to argue. If the cop could afford to stay at the Macdonald, he could afford to pay for his lunch.

Forty-nine

The day was pleasant and, except for his impatience, Jimmy enjoyed the walk, easily keeping pace with Pristupa's short, determined steps. It felt good to stretch his legs after so much sitting. Later on he would use the fitness facilities at the hotel. At least, that was the plan.

The Edmonton Times was located in a fairly new high rise with its offices located near the top. Never having visited a major newspaper office before, Jimmy was expecting something similar to what he'd seen in *All the President's Men*. But, of course, this was forty years later. White men in rolled-up shirtsleeves and suit pants had been replaced by a multi-ethnic, multi-gendered staff wearing casual clothing. Typewriters on desks had been replaced with computers in work stations separated by dividers high enough to allow for privacy. The main difference from *The Washington Post* as depicted in the film was the absence of noise. And no one was rushing around in a panic.

At the end of the room, a hallway led off to whatever else was necessary to produce the paper and keep the staff comfortable. Individual offices lined the outside wall of the building garnering windows for the editor and other senior staff. Pristupa knocked on a door marked "Sammy Greene, News Editor."

"It better be good," a gravel voice came from inside.

Pristupa chortled and opened the door. "I got something that'll tickle your fancy, Sam. But first, meet Detective Sergeant Jimmy Tan from Vancouver Island."

Greene's chair faced the window so the first thing Jimmy saw was the back of the man's head, which seemed to be covered with a solid clump of black and white hair. When he swivelled around, he revealed a deeply lined face framed by long protruding ears. His eyebrows were thick and black and hovered above hooded dark eyes. Charcoal crescents were carved on either side of his huge nose. Folds of skin drooped down on either side of his thin lips. He reminded Jimmy of a hound dog wearing a crocheted kippah.

"So, a cop from Lotus Land. To what do we owe the pleasure?" A tinge of acid coloured his words, and over his half-lens glasses he lasered a look at Jimmy.

"Now, Sammy. Don't be a nudnik," Pristupa uttered. "Show the man a little courtesy. He's here on a mission and he needs your help."

"*My* help? What kind of mission needs *my* help?"

"As it happens, he's investigating the murder of Elaine Monford."

"Ah." Greene's gaze softened. He quickly rose, offered Jimmy his bony hand, and just as quickly returned to his chair. "I was fond of that girl. She was meshugge. But funny. And interesting. Conversations with her were not your normal stock in trade. My door was always open to her." He glanced at Pristupa. "Unlike some others."

Pristupa said nothing, but his mouth twisted imperceptibly.

"And then she was gone. Fell off the Earth," Greene said dramatically.

"Our loss was her mother's gain," Pristupa said, the lie falling easily from his lips.

"Or so it seems." Greene stared at Pristupa a moment too long.

Jimmy wondered how much he knew.

"So, what is this thing that will tickle my fancy?"

"Well, I know I could find it if I did a search," Pristupa began. "But I'm sure you could pull the information out of that brain you've got buried under your yarmulke. Do you remember when a man came storming in, swearing that he was going to sue us because of something Elaine wrote about his daughter?"

Greene worked his tongue under his top lip as he looked away, thinking. Then he nodded. "As it happens, I do. It was before we moved here. Today he wouldn't have made it past the front desk. But in those days, you could walk in off the street and straight into the newsroom. The man could have killed Elaine if she'd been here and if he had half a mind to." He shuddered. "Good thing the other half had more sense."

"So, before 2004."

"Yes. There was something significant about the date." Folding his arms, he stared at the far wall, searching his memory.

On tenterhooks, Jimmy realized his body language must have signalled his edginess because Greene flashed him a look.

"*Hobn Geduld*. Have patience, young man. I just have to put myself back to that day so that I can see everything clearly. You understand?" Jimmy grunted an assent. "Good. So, there he is brandishing the newspaper and demanding to see the editor, yelling that he's going to sue the ass off the paper over a review and have Elaine in court for slander."

Pristupa jumped in. "Yeah. I remember now. I was in my office and came out when I heard the racket."

"You were the only one with an office back then, big shot."

Pristupa laughed. "Yeah. Now we're all equal."

"Some are more equal than others," Greene sparred.

Jimmy had just about had enough of their banter. "Could you just get to the point, please?"

Greene gave him a salty look, but relented. "Okay, okay. So we're all out there, watching this lunatic waving around the paper. I more or less ignored him because I knew what was in the article. I had blue pencilled out some words and told Elaine to make the corrections. I found them incendiary. "

"Obviously, if the man was breathing fire," Pristupa joked.

"So, now you're a comedian."

Jimmy, fearing another delay, cut in. "Would the review be in your archives?"

"It's in the archives of my brain, young man. The date was significant because it was the local auditions for the Metropolitan Opera. His daughter was one of the singers."

With this revelation, alarm bells began going off in Jimmy's head. "Do you remember her name?"

"I do. Elaine had done a take-off on her last name that was cruel. It was one of the things I told her to cut. The singer's name was Portman but Elaine used another word that was similar."

"Cripes!" Jimmy blurted.

The men stared at him. "I'm guessing this is important," Pristupa said.

"You remember me saying there was someone at the memorial service for Irina Stepanova who aroused my curiosity? Someone who thought she recognized Elaine Monford? It was Nadine Portman."

Greene's instincts as a former first-class newshound clicked in. "I'll retrieve that article." He turned around and got busy on his computer, humming as his fingers flew over the keyboard.

Jimmy sat down, his mind spinning. He knew the first thing he had to do was talk to Nadine Portman again to see if she had an alibi for the day of Elaine's murder.

Pristupa began to question Jimmy. "So this Nadine Portman has connections to that opera singer *and* Elaine. And if she recognized Elaine, do you think she might have accosted her?"

Before Jimmy could answer, Greene's humming stopped. "Here's the issue for that day." A few more seconds elapsed. "And here's her review. I'll print it out." A moment later, he pulled the page off the printer and handed it to Jimmy.

Painful. Painful. Painful. I'd rather have all of my teeth yanked out with no anaesthetic than sit through another day of warbling women. Or wobbling, in one case. When one particularly plump prima donna placed her hand on the piano, I thought it would collapse. Her name was Portman, but it should have been portly. It's true that it ain't over until the fat lady sings. But at least she had nice hair.

"Jesus." Jimmy's arm fell to his side. He looked up and through the window, not seeing the view, but envisioning the scene painted in the article.

Pristupa removed the paper from Jimmy's hand. As he read the words, his mouth tightened. "This is disgraceful. And this is supposed to be your edited copy?" He handed it to Greene, fury in his voice. "Look at this. You gave this your okay?" He plopped down on a chair.

Reading it, Greene blanched. "This was not the copy I approved, Henry. This is the first time I've seen the printed version." He spoke softly, almost to himself. "The little *klafte*. She went behind my back." He lowered his shaking head.

"And you didn't bother to read it when Mr. Portman arrived, threatening to sue you?" Jimmy asked incredulously.

"No," Greene said.

Pristupa looked down. "I'm ashamed to admit that I didn't, either. I just saw him as some disgruntled parent who thought we had done a disservice to his daughter. And, frankly, we had a newspaper to get out. He turned to Greene. "We both fell down on the job, Sam."

"For once, I agree with you."

Pristupa turned to Jimmy. "I could see where a person might wish someone dead over it, but to kill someone? It seems a pretty trivial reason to me."

"People commit murder for trivial things more often than you think," Jimmy said. Believing that he might now have to look at Nadine's father as the culprit, he needed to go back to square one.

Fifty

With the review tucked in his jacket pocket, Jimmy thanked them, then barreled out of the office, leaving the two newsmen to rehash history. He wasn't interested in how the unedited article landed up in the paper. His only interest now was the Portmans. If Nadine could account for her whereabouts on Easter weekend, then her father was next on the short list of suspects.

Arriving quickly at his hotel room, he logged on to his laptop to access her phone number. Expecting a message that the office was closed for the day, he was dismayed to hear that it was closed until after the Canada Day weekend, more than a month away. Anyone wishing to book an artist could call her on her private number. Of course, he wasn't privy to that number. Only those who were "in the know" would be able to reach her.

Issuing a mild oath, he logged onto the Canada 411 search site looking for a listing for Portman in Edmonton. There was a possibility that her parents knew where she was and how to reach her. Or she could even be in Edmonton, for that matter. And he might get a chance to interview the father as well. He tried alternative searches, but came up empty. There was no listing for a Portman, period. Perhaps they were like many people, disconnecting their land lines and using cellphones only. In a funk, he called home.

Ariel answered immediately. "Hello, there." The smile in her voice gave him a boost. "How are you?"

"Dumbstruck. And stuck, as a matter of fact."

"Dumbstruck? By what?"

"Turns out Nadine Portman had been a singer here years ago and she was viciously slagged by Elaine Monford."

"*She* was a singer?! You think it might be revenge after all? That she could have come back here and killed her after discovering who she was at the memorial service?"

"That's what I'm thinking. That's why I need to get an alibi from her. But her office is closed for over a month."

"Hmm. So she stopped singing and instead started a management company. How interesting." Ariel mused. "So why are you stuck?"

"I can't find a listing for her family. I was wondering if they might know where she is. I may have to bring in the RCMP for help. And they're going to want to know why. As soon as I mention the murder inquiry, they'll be all over me about jurisdiction. It'll be a hornet's nest."

She heard the exasperation in his voice. "But Jimmy, don't you already have a contact in Edmonton? That guy who came here. Remember? Why don't you see if he can do some sleuthing for you?"

Jimmy tapped his head in disgust. "Yeah. Of course. Dave Young. Why didn't I think of that? You're brilliant."

"No I'm not. I just remember things you tell me."

"Remind me to keep running off at the mouth. I don't have his contact numbers, but the chief does. I'll give him a call."

"Keep me posted."

"I will. I'll call you before I go to bed."

Chief Wyatt was sitting jawing with McDaniel and Novak when Mary-Beth informed him that Jimmy was on the line. "Tell him to hold on while I get to my phone." He pushed himself up from the armchair and lumbered into his office. As he did so, the two corporals glanced at each other with raised eyebrows. They became quiet, hoping to catch Wyatt's side of the conversation. Even Mary-Beth raised her built-in antennae.

Wyatt picked up the phone. "What's up, Tan?"

"Hi, Chief. Can you give me the number for Dave Young? I need his help."

"Why's that?"

Jimmy ran by the discovery of a stronger link between Monford and Portman and the urgent need to find her. Then he read the review to Wyatt.

"That's bloody awful," he uttered vehemently.

Mary-Beth, McDaniel and Novak straightened at the words. What was "bloody awful"?

"So maybe Monford *was* killed for something she wrote," the chief continued.

The eaves-droppers exchanged another glance.

"It's sort of looking that way. Anyway, I don't want to take another step until I talk to Dave Young. He may give me some advice on how to approach the Portmans. Or how to deal with the local detachment, if I have to do that."

"Yeah. You want to avoid stomping on anyone's corns. Hang on while I pull up the file." He put down the phone, then after a minute, picked it up. "Okay. Here we go. I've got two numbers for him. I would try his private line first."

As Jimmy wrote them down he heard Wyatt chuckling. "If the motive turns out to be as you say, Rossini is going to be royally pissed off." There was a beat and his tone darkened. "Christ. I hope we aren't going to need the Mounties to help close this case."

"I'll do what I can to avoid that, Chief." After ending the call, Jimmy took Wyatt's advice. The private line was answered on the first ring. "Dave Young." No rank or title.

Jimmy began to introduce himself, when he was interrupted.

"Hello there, Sergeant Tan. How are you and what can I do for you?" sounding almost glad to hear from him.

"I'm here in Edmonton, following up something that now seems like a legitimate lead in Elaine Monford's murder."

"Really? Well, I'll be more than happy to help in any way I can. If you *are* looking for help, that is."

"As a matter of fact, I am." Then for the third time that day, he related the essential parts of his investigation to Young, who waited until he was finished before saying anything. "I remember that review very well and reamed out Elaine over it. She shrugged it off. Said maybe she was doing the singer a favour and she'd go on a diet. So you're looking at Nadine Portman as a possible suspect here?"

"Unless there's a sister, because the Nadine Portman I saw in Britannia Bay certainly wasn't obese."

"Maybe she *did* go on a diet. Anyway, what can I do for you?"

After explaining what he needed and why, Young asked him what his next step would be if Nadine happened to be in Edmonton.

Jimmy hesitated. "I would want to talk to her. She may cooperate and I may get an alibi, or she might lawyer up, or worse, go to the very agency I am trying to avoid and complain of police harassment. If that happens, then I would have to explain my presence to the RCMP." He waited out the long silence.

"Hmm. That would open a territorial can of worms."

Jimmy's face felt hot. Maybe this had been a bad move.

"Let me see what I can do, Jimmy. Give me your cell number and I'll get back to you."

When he heard "Jimmy," he felt mildly relieved. Perhaps he hadn't overplayed his hand after all. He looked at his watch. "I'm going to try to get in a workout before dinner."

"Okay. I'll call just as soon as I have anything."

Feeling optimistic, Jimmy changed and descended into the bowels of the hotel. After a work-out and shower, he checked his messages. Nothing yet. Over dinner, he checked again. Still nothing. Back in his room, he put on the notification sound and got ready for bed. Seeing the time, he was certain he wouldn't be hearing from Young until the morning, so he called Ariel with an update.

"You'll just have to cool your heels, sweetheart. Get a good night's sleep and wait until he calls you. And if he and his contacts can't find her parents, all you can do is come home and wait until she returns to Toronto."

"I know you're right. But you're wrong about one thing."

"What's that?"

"There's no way I'll get a good night's sleep."

Fifty-one

The sun sent low shafts of light into the dining room as Jimmy ate his breakfast and read the complimentary edition of *The Edmonton Times*. There were only a few other diners—a quartet of American tourists preparing for an adventurous outing, a young couple smiling a great deal at each other across a table, and a few lone men. He had risen early with the hopes of finding a message from Dave Young, but on seeing nothing, he did what Ariel suggested—cooled his heels. His next move depended on what he heard from the CSIS operative.

The paper's editorial, no doubt written by Pristupa himself, bashed both the provincial and federal governments concerning their positions on a controversial oil pipeline. Having heard enough yesterday, he turned to the sports pages, wondering how the Toronto Blue Jays were doing, not because he was a sports fan, but because of Delilah's fanatical support of the team. She was always looking for a sympathetic ear and a chance to chat. They had won their last three games but were still in fourth place in their division. Maybe there was hope yet?

As he gulped down the last of his coffee, he felt his phone

vibrating. The display said, "Caller Unknown," but Jimmy guessed that it would be Young. He answered quietly.

"Good morning, Jimmy. I hope this is not too early."

Jimmy left his table, not wanting to be one of those people who thought nothing of carrying on a one-sided conversation in public. "Morning, Dave. No, I'm an early riser. Have you got anything?" He had reached the elevators and pressed the button for his floor.

"I do. But it's not going to help you much. Mrs. Portman sold the house four years ago and apparently doesn't live in Edmonton anymore."

"So, she was a widow?"

"Yes. Her husband, Ellis, died in 2010."

The name charged through Jimmy like an electric current. "Ellis?"

"That's right. Is that significant?"

"I think it's very significant. It throws a whole new light on the investigation. But whether it has anything to do with the murder I don't know."

"That sounds intriguing. Will you be on your way, then?"

"Yes. I'll be heading home on the first flight I can get."

Young picked up on the urgency in Jimmy's tone. "There's one in about an hour and a half, so I'll get off my horse and leave you to it. If there's anything else I can do, don't hesitate to ask."

"I will and thank you very much for this. I'll keep you informed."

"Thanks, Jimmy. I'd appreciate it. Bye for now."

Jimmy stepped into the elevator. The doors closed. And so did any speculation that Ellis Portman could have been responsible for Monford's death.

Driving to the airport, he got on his Blue Tooth and called the station. "Mary Beth, is Gene in yet?"

"Hi, Jimmy. Yes, he is. Just a sec."

Gene's resonant voice filled Jimmy's ear. "What's up, Sarge?"

"Go onto the website for Portman Artists' Management. What I want you to do is download the photographs of Nathalie Ellis and Nadine Portman, then pixilate them. I want to know if they could be one and the same person."

"Wow. Okay. Mysterious stuff. You still in Edmonton?"

"I'm on my way to the airport. I should be home by early afternoon. But if you get anything within the next forty-five minutes, phone me. After that, text, because I'll be on a plane."

"Roger. I'll get right on it."

"Thanks, Gene." Next, he called Ariel.

"Hi, sweetheart." Her morning voice warmed his heart.

"Hi, honey. I'm on my way to the airport. Dave Young gave me some information that shocked the hell out of me. Nadine Portman's father's first name was Ellis."

"As in *Nathalie* Ellis?"

"Yes."

"That's really weird. What's going on here?"

"I'm not sure, but I have Gene comparing the photographs of Nadine and Nathalie. You know, pixilating them to see if there's a possibility that they're the same person."

"Holy cow! What does all this mean?"

"I have no idea. But if we find out that it's true, we can check Nathalie Ellis's singing schedule and find out if she was somewhere else on Easter weekend. Maybe I won't have to contact Nadine Portman at all to get an alibi."

"But don't you want to know what the deception is all about? *I'm* certainly curious."

"That's not my business, Ariel. But if she can't provide a satisfactory alibi, then it *will* become my business."

"It would be easy enough to find out if she was singing somewhere. I can do that for you."

"Text me the answer. And Ariel, you're solid gold."

"I know."

Fifty-two

Jimmy blew through the station doors and came to a dead halt. Monique Stepanova sat in the foyer, a parcel on her lap. She stood, her face reflecting a combination of remorse and trepidation.

Holding out a battered brown folder, she stammered, "I—I found these papers in Irina's belongings. You need to read them. Well, the last one . . . especially. I think it points to who killed Diane Drake. I mean, Elaine Monford."

Jimmy's irritation bubbled to the surface. "Come with me," he said sharply.

Tamsyn Foxcroft looked up as he approached her work station and stole a quick peek at the woman in his wake.

"Tamsyn, are you tied up at the moment?"

Sensing his contained testiness, she bit back any smart remark. "Nothing that can't wait. What do you need?"

"Can you escort Mrs. Stepanova to Interview Room 1? I need to see McDaniel before I talk to her."

"Right." She got up and led the woman down the hall.

Monique was perplexed and annoyed. Wasn't he eager to find out what she had? She knew it was explosive. Maybe she should have been more forceful. Turning around to say something, she saw his back as he spoke to a Black policeman. Inwardly seething, she followed the First Nations officer into the sterile room and reluctantly sat at the appointed chair.

McDaniel headed to the incident room while Jimmy stopped at Wyatt's open door. "Chief, I have some new details about the Monford case. If you have a minute, can you join McDaniel and me?"

Wyatt nodded, rose, and gave hand-signals to Mary Beth as to where he would be.

McDaniel was seated in front of the monitors showing the original and pixilated pictures of Nadine Portman and Nathalie Ellis. "Here they are, Sarge." Jimmy and Wyatt peered at the screens. The similarities would have been difficult for most people to pick up as different hair colour, dark contact lenses and make-up application dramatically altered Nadine's appearance.

"That's it!" Jimmy shouted.

Wyatt and McDaniel shot startled looks at the normally placid cop.

"What's 'it'?" Wyatt asked.

"Her hair. I've been trying to remember what it was that Ariel and Mrs. Abernathy said about Nadine Portman. They commented on her hair. Even Elaine Monford mentioned it in her review in *The Edmonton Times*. Mrs. Abernathy said it was gorgeous." He pointed to the monitor on the left. "But *that* isn't gorgeous hair. Nadine Portman is wearing a blond wig." He then pointed to Nathalie Ellis on the right-hand monitor. "Now *this* is gorgeous hair. This is Nadine's *real* hair. She was wearing a hat when she came to the memorial service, but took it off at the Abernathy's."

"So, she's one and the same person," Wyatt said. "But what has this . . . charade got to do with the case?"

"At first glance, it doesn't seem to have anything to do with it. Maybe it began with her changing her last name, which Monford had mocked, and then she decided to go all out and change everything including losing a lot of weight. Ariel and I looked at the website for Nathalie Ellis, and her biography is almost a total blank. She's a mystery. Gene, print off the pictures of Portman and Ellis from the website."

"And do you still think it was murder?"

"I'm hedging my bets."

Gene handed him the print-outs. Jimmy tacked them to the whiteboard, bare but for a lone picture of Elaine Monford. Lastly, he wrote Irina Stepanova's name in the centre then drew lines from it to all three photographs.

"So, she's the link after all," Wyatt mused.

"She's central to this case. And now Monique Stepanova has come in with some papers from her mother-in-law's belongings. She thinks they point to a suspect."

Foxcroft closed the door behind her after Jimmy knocked and signaled for her to come out.

"Has she said anything?"

Tamsyn shook her head. "Not a word."

"Nothing?"

"Nope. Nada. She just sat there staring straight ahead."

"Did you say anything?"

"Nope. I matched her word for word," she smiled.

Jimmy chuckled. "Thanks, Tamsyn."

When he walked into the room, he noticed Monique's ramrod posture, hands still clasping the package on her lap. He sat across from her, taking in her piercing eyes. "You said you had documents that indicate a possible suspect in the death of Elaine Monford."

She placed the folder on the table. "These are letters written over many years between Nadine Portman and my mother-in-law."

"And what makes you think there is a suspect in them?"

"Do you know who Nadine Portman is?"

"Yes. I do."

Her surprise almost made Jimmy want to laugh. What did she think? That he was some kind of hick town cop?

Rather than say anything, she unwound the string between the two grommets and opened the brown accordion folder. Lifting out a packet of letters, she pulled out the last one. "Read this." She handed it to him.

Jimmy unfolded the letter, noted the date and began reading. Most of it was taken up with the Met regional auditions in Vancouver in 2010, which Nadine had won. The final paragraph, however, piqued his interest. He read: *Thank you so much for suggesting the visit to Heritage Gardens. We loved it.*

He mentally chastised himself for failing to ask Nadine Portman if she had ever been to Heritage Gardens. Not only had she been there, she had even stayed at the proprietor's bed and breakfast. But it was irrelevant at this stage. He already had what he needed, although he wondered who was included in the *"we"*. He folded the letter and placed it in front of Monique. "So you're suggesting that Nadine Portman was responsible for Elaine Monford's death?"

"It's obvious, isn't it? Nadine Portman had been to Heritage Gardens before. And she had a very good reason for taking revenge on Monford." She looked almost triumphal, waiting for Jimmy to ask why.

"You mean the review in *The Edmonton Times* when Monford publicly humiliated her?"

Monique's mouth dropped. "You know about that?"

"Yes. We also know that she performs as Nathalie Ellis."

The additional revelation stunned her.

"My question to you is, how long have *you* known this?"

Monique hesitated. "Not long."

"You know, of course, that it could have helped our investigation in the early stages. Because you failed to come to us with this information, you could be charged with obstructing justice."

Monique felt the moisture in her mouth dry up. She licked her lips several times before answering. "I . . . I wasn't sure how important it was until I reread them. I was more interested in how my mother-in-law helped transform Nadine into an opera star. The bit about Heritage Gardens didn't sink in."

"But you think Nadine Portman is guilty."

"I do."

"Well, as it happens. you are wrong. Nadine Portman was in Italy at the time of Monford's death."

"Oh, thank God!" she blurted.

Now it was Jimmy's turn to be surprised. "Why say, 'Thank God'?"

"Because I didn't want anything to happen to her career. She is an international star, and my mother-in-law was responsible for it. I didn't want either legacy to be tarnished."

"Is music so important to you that you would allow it to prevail over the death of someone?"

She straightened her shoulders, and set her flashing eyes on him. "It isn't simply *music*, Sergeant Tan. It's artistic talent of the highest calibre and difficult to achieve. To see it all come crashing down would have been a disaster. And for what? To assuage the death of a small-time, so-called critic who hadn't a smattering of musical knowledge? Who didn't understand the difference between Johannes Brahms and Bon Jovi? She was nothing compared to Nathalie Ellis. Nothing!"

Jimmy could feel the bile rising in his gorge. It was all he could do to control his breathing. He fell back on his martial art training to gather up the calm he needed at this moment. "Elaine Monford was much more than nothing, Miss Stepanova. As any human being is. No one is nothing. There is always a back story to every person's life—how they live and often how they die. There are circumstances that form us after birth. Some children are fortunate. Others are not. You cannot look at a person and think you recognize who they are. Most people would look at you and see a talented violinist who is dedicated to and perhaps loved by her students. I see a cold person with no empathy. There is no warmth in you. I doubt you were always this way. So there was something in your upbringing or perhaps later experiences that made you that way. I feel sorry for you." He pushed the letter across the table. "Now take your letters and leave."

Chafing under the rebuke, it took only a moment for her to collect herself. She snatched up the letters, stuffed them back in the folder, and stormed out the door.

Jimmy wished he could have arrested her and thrown her in their only cell. But he just wanted her out of his sight. Her visit had, however, thrown up another question—who was with Nadine on the visit to Heritage Gardens? And was it even relevant? It would have to remain a side story. The important determination was that Nadine was not responsible for Elaine's death, and that it was looking more and more like a botched robbery.

Exhaustion dropped down on him like an imploding tent. It had been a long day—another day with Ariel waiting for him. He hadn't been home since his return from Edmonton. Slowly pushing himself up, he walked back to the squad room and leaned wearily against Wyatt's door jamb. "Chief?"

A trace of a smile flitted across Wyatt's face. "Whatever it is, it can wait. Just go home. And Jimmy, good work."

"Thanks."

He stopped at Gene's work station, thanked him, then crossed the street to Bayside Foods. His remarkable and often-neglected wife deserved flowers—at the very least.

Fifty-three

W hat're you apologizing for this time, Jimmy?" Barb asked, her raspy voice now a thing of the past. More than one customer had complained about the smell of tobacco emanating from the long-time smoker. Management took her aside. Either quit smoking or work in the cold storage warehouse a couple of miles out of town. Giving up her customer contact would be worse than giving up the smokes. She quit.

"Been gone a couple of days, Barb."

"Ariel will love these. They're beautiful. I see you're learning." She took the selection of Star Gazer and Casablanca lilies and wrapped them. She held out her hand. "Where's the card?"

"Oh. I forgot." Jimmy realized he had failed once again. He glanced behind him. "I don't want to hold up the line."

Barb frowned. "You disappoint me, Jimmy. And you were doing so well." She looked at the waiting customers. "You don't mind while this nice young man selects a card for his wife, do you? He has trouble doing more than one thing at a time." She turned back to him. "Find a pretty one. And write something nice," she admonished.

Everyone laughed. People often waited in her line even though other cashiers were free. They always left feeling happier and sometimes came away with a bit of gossip. It was a toss-up which one they preferred.

Jimmy blushed as he walked quickly to the kiosk and selected a card with no verse. He brought it back. "I'll write something nice," he said, causing more chuckling down the line.

Approaching the house, Jimmy heard cursing in the garden. He found Ariel standing beside her berry patch, deer netting and poles tangled in a heap on the ground. "God damn deer! God damn deer!" The plants had been trampled or torn out.

She saw Jimmy out of the corner of her eye and turned toward him, anguish and anger on her face. "Look what they've done! The strawberries are toast. There isn't a ripe raspberry left." A kind of helplessness tinged her voice. Her last, "God damn deer!" was subdued.

The flower beds had been sectioned off with high poles and plastic netting like individual prison cells. So far the animals hadn't bothered them. But berries were irresistible. "I'm sorry, Ariel. I'll help you get the fencing back up and we can put more poles in."

She managed a smile. "Thank you, and welcome home." He held out the bouquet. "Oh, these are absolutely beautiful! You sweetheart." She kissed him. He handed her the envelope. "And a card, too? You've only been gone two days."

"It seemed longer."

"Yes. But it was worth it, wasn't it?"

He nodded. "It was." They were walking toward the patio doors. The cats, having fled upon hearing Ariel's loud invectives, appeared out of nowhere and darted along in front of them. Jimmy squatted down. "Roger," he called. The cat ran back, rubbed his cheeks against Jimmy's fist a couple of times then bounded through the open door.

Later that evening, the lilies were already beginning to fill the house with their heady scent, almost overpowering the fennel and garlic in Ariel's pork daube casserole. Sitting at the kitchen table, refreshed and fed, Jimmy told her about Monique and the letter from Nadine mentioning the visit to Heritage Gardens.

"What!? She had been there before and didn't tell you?"

"I didn't even think to ask," he admitted, shaking his head.

"But since she has an alibi it doesn't matter anyway, does it?"

"No."

"It's kind of a strange coincidence, though, don't you think?"

"Mm-hmm. And another strange coincidence is her staying at Charterhouse. When she made the reservation, she couldn't have known that Abernathy was also President of Heritage Gardens. And if I know him, he would've found an opportunity to brag about that. I wonder what her reaction would've been."

"Well, she didn't have any worries there. He didn't arrive on the scene until some time after her tour with Irina. So he wouldn't have recognized her. Moreover, he normally doesn't have any interaction with visitors, unless it's a VIP."

"It would have satisfied my curiosity to know who was with her and Irina that day. You know, the mysterious *we*. But I doubt it would've been anyone who had a reason to kill Elaine Monford."

"It would more than likely have been her mother who was with them. But if it *was* a murder, can you see a woman, who's probably in her sixties, carrying it off?"

"No. That would be stretching it," he agreed.

"Are you going to close the case now?"

He shrugged. "I'll leave that decision to the Chief. But I expect that's what'll happen."

"But you aren't satisfied, are you?"

"No." Then he smiled. "Am I ever?"

"Do you think the trip to Edmonton was a waste since it seems it might have been a botched robbery after all?"

"Most detective work *is* a waste, honey. But you have to do it anyway, just to make sure it isn't a waste."

"It's all so strange, though. This subterfuge. The ruse by everyone involved. She had help, of course. It would have been impossible to pull off on her own. Why did they do it? Why was it necessary?"

"We'll never know, Ariel. People do strange things when it comes to their public persona. A lot of times it skirts the truth. Or is made up." He looked at her levelly. "Just think about mine."

Silence slipped into the space where she might have replied. Everything stilled. Only the gentle ticking of the grandmother clock suggested the passing of time.

Jimmy yawned. "Come on, honey. Let's clean up and call it a day."

"Hmm. Can we call it a day and clean up later?"

There was no mistaking the intimation in her voice.

Fifty-four

June 9ᵗʰ

There could have been a parade. The excitement had been building ever since Ray and Georgina, *sans* Gabriella, returned home. Georgina had immediately swung into action, putting the finishing touches on their renovated restaurant. Piqued by a full-page article in *The Bugle,* people had been hoping to peer inside the new patio doors and windows to see the changes, but they were thwarted by the heavy brown paper blocking their view. The newspaper had been no help as it had been prevented from taking photographs of the interior. It was all very hush-hush. The only thing anyone knew for sure was the opening date.

Ray, himself, hadn't been involved in any of the last-minute details. His own newly renovated rear-end was happily settled in his chair at the station. When he had arrived, his waistline wasn't at first apparent as his arms were laden with gifts. But after unloading the boxes and bags, he stood in his new Italian suit looking like the "after" picture of a weight-loss clinic ad. The change was startling.

"Eh, goomba, what happened to you?"

"I'll tell you what happened, Novak. I ate real Italian food. And lots of it. No crap. I walked everywhere. I must've walked ten, fifteen miles every day. The only time I sat was when I ate." He opened his jacket, patted his flat stomach and puffed out his chest. "I'm a new man."

But only in appearance. He was still the same old Ray, and a welcome sight. Although Jimmy had enjoyed a lot of his solitary sleuthing, he realized he had missed the back and forth with his partner. Of course, the first thing Ray wanted to discuss was the Monford case. Jimmy was prepared.

"I'm guessing you didn't find a person with a plausible motive for murder."

"You'd be guessing right."

"So it's down as a botched robbery."

Jimmy nodded.

"And the case is closed."

"Yep."

"Good. Anything else shaking?"

"Nope."

Ray leaned back in his chair and sighed. "*Bene. Bene. La vita è bella.*"

Lana followed a few days after the Rossinis, stopping at Ariel's after a tour of the refurbished restaurant. She, too, had come bearing gifts, along with her tablet holding an abundance of photographs. After both had been dealt with, she got to the news.

"There's going to be a new second chef at Catalani's, and he's a bit of a dish himself."

Ariel's eyes lit up. "Ooh. What's his story?"

"His name is Stefano Moretti. He was head chef for one of the remaining members of the House of Savoy. I guess there was some sort of falling out and he wound up in Pesaro working in Leonora's restaurant. That's where Gabriella has been learning the local cuisine.

Apparently he sort of adopted her—took her under his wing. And by the way, Gabby's not coming back until the fall. Or even later."

"She's not? What happened?"

"She just fell in love with the place and the people."

"She hasn't fallen in love with Stefano, has she?"

"Oh, no. He's far too old for her. I think she's checking out the *ragazzi*. Some of them are drop-dead gorgeous."

"Hmm. Yeah. George Clooney comes to mind. I'm guessing Russell Martin is long gone."

"Gone with the wind."

"How did Stefano wind up coming here?"

"Ray and Georgina were quite taken with him and after getting to know him better, they asked if he would be interested in working at Catalani's. After Stefano spoke to Leonora he was sold on Britannia Bay. The paperwork is already in the pipeline."

"When do you think this dish will arrive so we can get a good look at him?"

"You don't have to wait. I just happen to have a few photos." She pulled out her cellphone and showed Ariel pictures of him with Rossini family members and one with Lana.

"Yum. He really *is* a dish."

"As for when he'll arrive, I'm not sure. But certainly not by opening night. By the way, I checked the reservation list and you and Jimmy are on it."

Ariel clasped her hands and bowed.

Lana hoped she had steered the conversation away from Stefano. She feared any further talk would trip her up and reveal her feelings. On the day they met, their halting introductions in garbled Italian and English had them laughing. He had instinctively touched her arm as if it were the most natural thing in the world to do. For Lana, it was an instant connection that felt more mental than physical, and it set her emotions rolling. How was she going to chart her course now? Georgina had been busily going through the reservation requests and it was clear that the restaurant would be filled to capacity on opening night even before half the list had been winnowed. She had to include certain individuals, but kept some of the politicians and other titled freeloaders out. Wanting to make it more of an evening for friends and colleagues, she made sure that Ray's "asks" were included.

Returning calls required all her diplomatic skills in suggesting another evening or lunch. Some were mollified, understanding the situation. Others were incensed. She made a note of their names and began a black list. In future, a table would "regretfully" not be available for them on the day and time they wanted. At last the seating was settled. Now all she had to do was audition the wait staff that had been hired by a professional agency, give them a transliteration of the Italian, and have them learn what was in each dish. That was all? she thought. It would be the most time consuming, and a possible minefield.

She was glad about one thing: Stefano wouldn't be arriving for a few weeks. He could easily be a distraction with his charming manner and good looks. She wanted her female staff in the dining room. Not hovering about the kitchen hoping for a glance from his dark eyes. Was hiring him a mistake? *Can't worry about that now. We'll just have to see what happens.* What she did not know was that it had already happened.

Fifty-five

The Following Saturday Morning

Jimmy and Ariel looked at their handiwork. It had required all their efforts to return the garden to its former self. For three days they had worked, replacing the poles with ones that were stronger and reattaching the netting. When it was complete, Ariel remarked that it still looked like a prison.

"There's no other solution, Ariel. We can't put a barrier around the entire property."

"Oh, I know that. But it's so discouraging." She gave a sign of frustration.

"There's one upside to it, though."

"What's that?" she asked, her skepticism apparent.

"It keeps the cats from using the garden as one giant litter box."

Ariel rolled her eyes then tapped him in the arm. "Let's go in. I'm starving."

After lunch they lingered at the table enjoying their usual Saturday pastime—at least Jimmy was. "I've finished the puzzle. How're you doing?"

"As a matter of fact, I haven't looked at it yet. I've been working on an anagram." She handed him a sheet of paper.

He read *Elaine Monford*. Underneath, Ariel had rearranged the name into an Italian phrase.

"I get the last word, but what does the first word mean?" Jimmy asked.

"'Dying.' In music, it means to die away before the end."

The irony was not lost on them.

Epilogue

Santa Fe, New Mexico

The air-conditioned tour behind the scenes at Santa Fe Opera had been a welcome respite in the morning's searing heat. Although fun and informative, the walkabout was a little longer than Grant's aching back could take. He was relieved when Belle and Nadine finally suggested a late lunch. Arriving at La Plazuela, he sagged into the comfortable chair and gave a long sigh.

Belle laughed. "Too much for you, darling?"

He moved his head side-to-side and rolled his eyes. "I was fine until we got to the costume department. Bo-ring."

"I loved it!" Belle enthused. "It was fascinating to see how they adjust a garment to fit different builds."

"I didn't see any for the famous fat lady," Grant chuckled, unaware that he was touching on a sensitive subject.

Nadine exchanged a meaningful look with her mother. "There really aren't many like that these days, Grant. Especially after Covent Garden cancelled one famous diva's contract because she couldn't get into a particular dress. I think it alerted singers to go easy on the pasta."

"Speaking of food," Grant said, picking up a menu. Their conversation changed to matters at hand as they scrutinized the appetizers and entrees then placed their order.

"I'll tell you one thing I *did* find interesting, though," Grant said, looking at Nadine. "Hearing all those people calling you Nathalie or Miss Ellis. I know it's your stage name, but it took me a minute."

Belle laughed. "That's fame, Grant," she said, then turned to her daughter. "I actually wondered if the make-up artists would recognize you without your long hair. When I saw all those wigs, I could understand why you had it cut. It must've been hot under the stage lights."

Nadine unconsciously touched her short bob. "It was. And stuffing it under the wigs could be a chore for the Wig Assistants. It was easier with the elaborate hair styles of period operas, but some roles call for short hair. Like *Lulu.*"

"Oh, that ghastly opera! All that sex and violence. Not to mention the awful music."

"Even so, the performances are almost always sold out."

"Sex and violence? No wonder," Grant said.

The waiter arrived with their appetizers, which they shared.

"What do you want to do later on?" Nadine asked between bites.

Grant groaned. "If we're gonna do anything else, I'll have to take a nap first."

Belle shook her head, smiling. She turned to Nadine. "Well, I'd like to find a cool place where I can go for a run—" she began.

"Naturally," he cut in. "It doesn't matter where we are. Belle has to find a place to go biking or running."

"Well, it's far easier to do that than find a gym where I can box," she said testily.

Nadine looked at her mother with surprise. "Are you still boxing?"

"Oh, yes. I kept it up after Ellis died."

Nadine remembered how her father had taken up boxing when he contracted Parkinson's. And how Belle, inspired by his improvement, took to sparring with him.

"She packs a mean punch, I can tell you," Grant laughed, playfully rubbing his jaw.

Belle lay awake reliving those few days in April when she was on her own, free to do the one important thing waiting at the bottom of her bucket list. When Nadine had first called with the news that Elaine Monford might be in Britannia Bay, the ashes of rage that had been lying dormant in Belle caught fire. Later, when Nadine mentioned that the reporter might be responsible for Irina's death, the hatred harboured in Belle's heart was fed by grief—grief that the person who had rescued and transformed her daughter had been scorned by a nobody trying to be a somebody.

Upon learning that Elaine would be covering an evening event at Heritage Gardens on Easter weekend, Belle saw a way to put everything right. The timing was fortuitous. Grant would be in Fort MacMurray. She could drive the motorhome to Vancouver, where she would meet up with him before their trip to U.S. But first she would take a side trip of her own—back to Heritage Gardens. This time, however, it wouldn't be for cream tea.

The logistics had been formidable, but she had carried it off. After three days in Britannia Bay, she had two plans in place. On the night, there had been one heart-stopping moment, and one factor that might have dashed her chosen scheme. Then the stars had aligned in her favour. With fortune and the element of surprise on her side, all it had taken was a few words, one grab, one punch, and it was done.

Afterwards, she did a mental check. How did she feel? Fine. How was her conscience? Clear. It had taken years, but it was done. Seeing Nadine on stage was all the proof Belle needed that the wait had been worth it.

ACKNOWLEDGMENTS

First, a huge thank you to Dianne Kennedy for her meticulous editing of the first draft. No easy task. Second, hats off to La Vernne Miller for pointing out correct antecedents, proper comma placement and other grammatical slips. These two remarkable women are, however, not responsible for any errors or omissions that might pop off the page because, after I received their proofed manuscripts, I added new material, which I did not resubmit for their corrections. Therefore, any mistakes are mine. Finally, my gratitude to Bryce Gibney for valuable research material, and to the following who gave suggestions for the back cover blurb: Julia DeVoretz, Ruth Findlay, Dianne Kennedy and Carol Oosthuizen, and to Ann Lemieux, who pared it down and made it work.

To my readers: If you enjoy anagrams, you may want to solve the one involving the name Elaine Monford. Ariel has already given you a hint.

Please visit my website at sydneypreston.com